Dance with Me

A
California Belly Dance Romance
Novel

Book 2

Dance with Me

A
California Belly Dance Romance
Novel

Book 2

DEANNA CAMERON

Fine Skylark Media
California

This book is a work of fiction. Names, characters, places, and incidents are products of the author's imagination or are used fictitiously. Any resemblance to actual persons, events, or locales is entirely coincidental.

Fine Skylark Media
P.O. Box 1505
Lake Forest, California 92609-1505

Cover photography by Vintra via Depositphoto.com (dancer) and Illustrated Romance (male model)

TITLES BY DEANNA CAMERON

The Girl on the Midway Stage
(previously published as *The Belly Dancer*)
The Girl on the Vaudeville Stage
(previously published as *Dancing at The Chance*)
Shimmy for Me
Dance with Me
Another Dance
Jingly Bells

PRAISE FOR *SHIMMY FOR ME*

"DeAnna Cameron delivers satisfying happily ever afters that will leave you sighing."
—Beth Yarnall author of *Wake Up Maggie*

"Cameron ensures that love triumphs in a delightful and believable way."
—Susan Squires, New York Times bestselling author of the Magic series

PRAISE FOR *THE BELLY DANCER*

"A beautifully written page-turner with characters that leap off the page, *The Belly Dancer* transports readers into an exotic and sensual world within a world, as plucky but initially naive Dora Chambers fights Chicago society's conventions and her husband's indifference to discover, in the thrall of the Egyptian Theatre, a passion beyond her wildest dreams."
—Lynette Brasfield, author of *Nature Lessons: A Novel*

"The 1893 World's Fair was a marvel, and in her debut, Cameron uses this backdrop to demonstrate one woman's view of herself. Society is forever altered because of what she learns in the lush, sensual, and exotic world of belly dancers. With a strong and vibrant picture of the era and a feminist approach to history, Cameron makes statements about women's rights and society's constraints."

—RT Book Reviews (4 stars)

PRAISE FOR *DANCING AT THE CHANCE*

"Old New York comes to vibrant life in this dazzling tale of follies and illusions. *Dancing at The Chance* serves up a racy, exuberant feast for the senses, with a lively and intrepid heroine determined to succeed in a fading world threatened by fast-paced, fickle modernity."

—C.W. Gortner,
author of *The Confessions of Catherine de Medici*

"*Dancing at The Chance* took me back to Old New York, when vaudeville still enchanted audiences and Ziegfeld was king. In her second novel, DeAnna Cameron brings the world of 1900's theatre to vibrant life. Part circus, part Shakespeare, part Arabian nights, the Chance Theatre is a place I would love to visit again."

—Christy English, author of *To Be Queen*

DEDICATION

To Austin and Chloe

CHAPTER ONE

THE MAN IN a vintage tuxedo gazed down at the belly dancer with bedroom eyes and crooned as she pressed her shimmies against him. A warm flush came over Melanie, as though she were intruding on a private moment, not one played out for a movie camera more than sixty years ago.

"Aren't those black-and-white films great?"

Melanie spun away from the television at the sound of her friend's voice and nearly knocked a box of hip scarves off the glass display case. She adjusted it back in place and composed herself.

"Sorry." Abby snickered. "I didn't mean to startle you."

"You didn't," Melanie grumbled, returning to her task of folding the scarves into tidy squares and stacking them beside the cash register. "I thought you were in the dance room, helping Janaya with the class."

"She wants to try teaching on her own." Abby grabbed a bag of chandelier earrings that needed to be organized.

Melanie's eyes widened. "It's only her second week. Is she ready?"

Abby shrugged and continued hanging the dangling earrings on the revolving floor stand. "We won't know till she tries. Honestly, I'm happy for the break. I feel guilty leaving you up here to work on the boutique by yourself. You should at least let me pay you."

"No way. After all the free studio time you've given me, it's the least I can do. Besides, the less time I have to spend at my mom's place, the better."

"So what's that like, living with your mom again?"

"Hell." Behind her the musical number on the screen came to an end, leaving a silence in the shop that made her uneasy. She turned and clicked off the television, happy to do anything but meet the questions she knew she'd find in her friend's expression, if she dared to look.

"What happened between you and Chet anyway?"

There it was, the question she'd been avoiding all week.

"You know, the usual," she mumbled and grabbed another wad of chiffon and jingly beads from the box. As she folded the chiffon with laser-sharp focus, her arms prickled from Abby's glare. She peeked upward.

Abby was not only staring, but her lips were tucked in that stubborn expression that said she was not going to let the topic go.

"It didn't work out," Melanie said, feeling partly ashamed and partly irritated. "It wasn't anyone's fault. It was just over. Where should I put these?" She held out the stack of neatly folded scarves like an offering.

"That shelf," Abby said, pointing to the far wall. "Next to the veils. Were you the one who broke it off?"

Melanie finished arranging the scarves and tossed the empty box across the room. She frowned at the pile of them mounting in the doorway. "I should probably take those out to the trash bin."

Abby folded her arms over her chest, obscuring most of the hot-pink "Shimmy Shop" logo she had screened onto teeny-tiny black camisoles. Her personal version of a uniform. "Uh-uh, you're not going to change the subject this time. Tell me what happened."

Melanie sighed. She ran a perfectly shaped red fingernail along her bottom lip to fix a nonexistent lipstick smudge, patted the tube curl of her honey-brown bangs, and nudged the scarlet silk rose over her ear. Yeah, she was stalling. What was the point of hurrying when she knew whatever she said next would be followed by a lecture?

Abby still had that look.

"Here's the thing," Melanie said. "I'm happy to help you get the boutique ready, but can we cut the talk about ex-boyfriends? It's kind of a buzzkill."

Abby shook her head. "Oh, no. Not when he just became an ex-boyfriend a week ago. After two years together, you better believe you are not getting off that easy."

"What?" Melanie cried. "Chet and I were together for a year. A year and a half, tops."

"I was talking about you and me, bonehead. We've been friends for two years." She waved her fingers at Melanie. "You wouldn't let me get away with that crap. So spill."

Melanie leaned back against the counter and stared out the plate-glass window that looked onto the parking lot. "It wasn't a big deal. He just got too serious."

"Serious? How serious? Did he propose?"

Melanie could hear the excitement in Abby's voice. Why did females always get batshit crazy when you mentioned marriage?

"Holy crap. He proposed and you dumped him?"

Why did it sound so much worse when Abby said it? It didn't matter. Once she got past this conversation, she never had to talk about it—or think about it—again. "I told him from the beginning I didn't plan to get married. I don't want kids, I don't want any of it. I was honest."

"I know, but c'mon," Abby said. "I didn't think I wanted those things either, but then I met the right guy, we started spending time together, and nature took its course."

Melanie blinked hard, stopping the eye roll that ached to be rolled. "Maybe for you," she said. "Don't get me wrong. I'm happy for you. If Derek makes you happy and you want that 'till death do you part' thing, great. It's just not for me. There are too many places I want to go, and too many things I want to do. Tying myself down to one person for the rest of my life just isn't one of them."

Abby cocked her head. "This is because of Belly Dance Divas, isn't it? Was he trying to talk you out of auditioning?"

"It doesn't matter." Melanie wiped imaginary dust off the counter. "The important thing is now I'll have more time to rehearse. After work, before work—if Deffner isn't watching, maybe during work, too."

"As if you need it," Abby said. "I don't know anyone who puts in more hours on the dance floor than you."

Melanie forced a smile. "If only that were enough."

"What do you mean?"

"Never mind," she said.

"So does that mean the geisha girl tattoo is off?"

"Yeah, that's history," Melanie said.

Actually, that was the hardest part of the breakup. Losing a boyfriend was one thing, but losing out on free ink from one of the best tattoo artists in Orange County was another. She rubbed at the mehndi-style lotus he'd given her on her last birthday. A tribal-inspired match for the rose and hibiscus flowers she'd gotten as a high school graduation present to herself.

He'd promised a geisha girl on her back to tie into the cherry blossoms on her thigh for her birthday, but that was still months away. Even if she offered to pay, that deal was more than likely off the table.

A blur of motion in the parking lot caught her eye. She watched a blazing yellow Porsche coupe screech to a halt.

"Uh-oh," she said. "Here comes trouble."

CHAPTER TWO

TAZ ROMAN PULLED his Porsche 911 Carrera S into the dance studio's parking lot and killed the engine. He sat, paralyzed. His sister's words swarming around in his brain like angry bees.

"You need to settle down," she pressed through the Bluetooth speaker. "You need to have some focus in your life and grow up. You're not a kid anymore. By the time Dad was your age, he had a whole orchestra. He and Mom were at the height of their careers."

"What's your point?" Taz growled.

"That you're wasting your time with the Belly Dance Divas. You're the best thing in that show. You're a Roman. You should be the headliner."

He touched his temples and stared into the glare of sunlight glancing off the car's hood. He measured his words carefully. "You haven't even seen the show."

"I don't have to. How could I, knowing you were so close to striking out on your own? But you had to go and let that snake Garrett weasel his way into the deal—"

"You don't know what you're talking about." His heart thumped the way it always did when they argued. He tried to be calm. He tried to breathe. He tried not to care.

"Don't I?" she needled. "I know what I see when I look at a Belly Dance Divas poster: I see his name splashed over everything, like he's the reason the show's so successful."

Taz closed his eyes and took a deep breath. "My name is there, too."

"It's at the bottom. Underneath the dancers. I guess that shouldn't surprise me. From what I hear, you're beneath quite a few of those dancers these days. No wonder—"

"Enough," he said, his knuckles burning white on the steering wheel. "Stop pretending you're my mother. Just because she's gone"—after all these years he still couldn't bring himself to say *dead*— "doesn't mean you get to fill the spot."

There was a silence. Then a meek, "I'm sorry. I just worry about you. When I was there, I knew what was happening. You said you'd come to New York to visit, but you haven't come since the wedding. It's been two years. You can't blame me for worrying about my little brother, especially when I hear what's happening with the show and these girls."

"You don't have to worry," he said. "It's a good show, and I'm in a good spot, whether you want to believe it or not."

"But you need someone to take care of you. You need someone who understands you and your talent and can look out for you. Someone like Tamara, who—"

"Stop," he blurted. He wasn't going to think about her. Not now. Not ever. He'd walled off that part of his life a long time ago. It was better that way.

Gina perked. "Oh?"

In that one syllable, he heard the conversation pivot.

"Is there someone new?" she coaxed. "Someone special?"

There wasn't anyone remotely close, but he heard opportunity in her tone. If he told her the truth, she'd go right back to haranguing him. But if he didn't…

"Yeah," he lied. "I've met someone new."

"Why didn't you say so? Do I know her? Is it serious? How serious?"

Even with three thousand miles between them, her giddiness radiated loud and clear.

"Well, you know…" He cracked a grin, relieved to be off the defensive.

"It is serious. I can hear it. I want to meet her. You know what?"

He heard the flutter of papers at the other end of the connection. "Todd's going to a work conference next week, so I'm coming to California. No reason to stay in this penthouse all alone for a week, not when I can spend quality time with my little brother and his new girlfriend."

Sudden panic set in. "You can't," he said.

"Why not? I'll stay in my old room. It'll be just like old times." She paused. "Unless she's living with you. Is she living with you? She is! You devil! You should have said so."

He made a face. Was this getting better or worse? "I didn't want to say anything until—"

"Until you knew it was going to work out. I get it. Well, I'm sure it'll be fine. It'll be better than fine. It'll give me a chance to get to know... what's her name, anyway?"

He froze. Then he said the only thing he could think to say. "What?" he bellowed. "You're breaking up. I'm losing the signal. Are you still there?"

She repeated herself, but he wasn't listening. He tapped the phone's screen and ended the call. Then he tore away the Bluetooth ear piece and threw it against the windshield.

What the hell had he just done?

CHAPTER THREE

MELANIE PUT DOWN the scarf she was folding and stared out the window again at the yellow Porsche. "Is he just going to sit there?"

"What do you care?" Abby asked, her head buried in a box of circle skirts. "I thought you couldn't stand him."

"I don't care. It's just weird. Sitting out there when it's got to be ninety degrees. Whatever happened to June Gloom? This heatwave sucks."

"Maybe he's on the phone. Maybe he's talking to Garrett about the tour." She stood up and gave Melanie a long, loaded look. "Or maybe they're talking about the auditions. You know, you might want to be nicer to him this time. He might be one of the judges."

The car door swung open and Melanie saw his shoulder-length mane of tawny-brown hair emerge first. Then the rest of his lean, six-foot-and-change frame appeared. A leg clad in distressed jeans, slung low and snug on his narrow hips. A tanned and rippled chest flashing through a white, open shirt. A chest that was nearly as famous as his talents with a drum.

Melanie dropped her glance to the new batch of scarves and tried to ignore the jingle of the bell when he opened the door.

"Taz, it's great to see you," Abby said, sliding aside the mountain of empty boxes blocking him from the boutique. "What brings you by?"

Melanie nearly gagged. Abby was laying it on thick. Just because he strutted around like some kind of celebrity didn't actually make him one. She stared harder into the mound of chiffon.

"You said you'd like to stock the Belly Dance Diva CDs in your shop, so I brought you a box."

You'd think he was doing them a favor, not the other way around. What a jerk. It was always the same with hot guys. They look good, but their attitudes suck.

Abby didn't seem to notice or care. "Absolutely," she said cheerfully, relieving him of the box he had tucked under his arm. "I'm so glad you remembered. We're hoping to open in a couple weeks, and I know these will go fast. Some of the students are already asking about them."

"I also snuck in a stack of Pandemonium Ball flyers. It's almost sold out, but there might be a few tickets still around, if anyone's interested."

"Are you going?" Abby asked.

He nodded. "The Divas are cosponsoring this year, so I'll be playing. You going?"

"I wish," Abby said. "All my money's going into this place, but I'm hoping to attend next year."

"Yeah," he said. "You should. It's a good time." He scanned the room, taking in the stacks of boxes, and the shelves slowly filling with merchandise. "Your place is looking really good. Are you planning something for the grand opening? I heard the showcase last month was a big hit. I'm sorry I missed it. Did it..."

What he was trying to ask without actually asking was obvious. Why did that kind of cowardly hesitation always annoy the hell out of her?

"The bank won't be swooping in to close her down any time soon," she blurted, "if that's what you mean."

Abby shot her a horrified look. Taz looked at her like she'd materialized out of thin air.

"What she means is," Abby continued, "the studio's business is great, and it will get even better as soon as I can find a day manager to oversee the boutique and our online shop."

Down the hall, the dance room door opened, followed by a stampede of bare feet and dance shoes. Melanie checked the wall clock. It was break time for the class. She braced herself for what was coming.

Then, right on cue, a squeal: "Taz!" A girl with a curly mop of red hair rushed up to him. "Oh my God, Taz Roman, what are you doing here?"

Curly was quickly joined by a dozen of the girls and women who made up the Saturday morning belly dance class.

Sheesh. You'd think he was Brad Pitt for belly dancers.

When he explained he was dropping off CDs, it set off another round of squeals. "If we buy one, will you sign it?"

"Of course," he said, with that toothy celebrity smile of his. "I'd love to."

That was an understatement. You could see it in the way he basked in the adoration. Puh-leez.

"Ladies, let's give him some room. Okay, who wants one?" Abby counted the hands—which was all of them—and pulled out fourteen CDs. "He'll sign them and then you can pay after class. You don't want to waste your class time." She exchanged a look with Janaya, who was an accomplished performer but was obviously still learning how to keep a class full of pheromone-surging females under control.

To his credit, Taz worked fast, and he charmed every one of those giggling students as he did it.

When they were finished and back in the dance room, Abby gathered up the CDs and set them beside the cash register.

"That was very generous of you," she said to Taz. "You made their day. Didn't he, Melanie?" She bumped Melanie with her hip when she didn't get a response.

"Hey! Ow. I mean, yeah, that was pretty cool of you." She made a face at Abby.

Taz didn't seem to notice. He was standing at the window, staring at the parking lot.

"Actually, they made mine," he said. "It's been an epically bad day so far."

"Girl trouble?" Melanie asked with a smirk. It was supposed to be a joke because—c'mon, this was Taz the Romancer. Everyone knew the only trouble he had with girls was fitting them all into his limited schedule.

So it took her by surprise when he said, "Yeah, you could say that."

"Seriously?"

Abby slanted her a hard look that screamed, "Shut up."

"I'm sorry to hear that," Abby said, using her sweetest, most sympathetic voice. "I didn't know you were seeing someone."

He ran his fingers through his hair, brushing it back over his shoulder. "I'm not. It's my sister."

Melanie choked. Not a small, polite hiccup, but something loud and nearly obscene. Abby just stared.

"That came out wrong," Taz said, almost laughing. "I'm not seeing anyone, but my sister thinks I am. Now she's coming out to meet her."

"To meet the girlfriend who doesn't exist?" Melanie asked.

He nodded. "I know it sounds ridiculous, but she's been on my case about everything lately, including settling down. She misunderstood something I said. It just seemed easier to let her believe I had met someone. Until she said she was coming out to meet the mystery girl. Now I don't know what I'm going to do."

"You could try telling her the truth," Abby offered.

"I know. I should," he said. "And I will. I'm just not in a big hurry. She's difficult under the best of circumstances. This is going to—"

"I don't see the big deal," Melanie interrupted.

Two pairs of eyes shot her direction.

"What? Like you couldn't find someone in a heartbeat who was willing—eager even—to pretend she was your girlfriend?"

His expression twisted. "Yeah, maybe too eager. I wouldn't want to give someone the wrong idea, even if she was doing me a favor. Besides, she'd have to be convincing. My sister's pretty sharp. She's got the brains in the family."

That wasn't a surprise.

"But," Abby said, "what if this mystery girl were getting something in return?" She turned to Melanie.

Instinctively, Melanie shook her head. She didn't know what was brewing beneath that black ponytail, but she knew that devious look. She knew that tone.

Abby continued. "If she were getting something in return, she'd be motivated to make it convincing."

Taz looked curious or confused—it was hard to say which. "Something like what?"

Crap. Melanie's heart raced, and her palms burned. She would have made a run for it if there wasn't an obstacle course of boxes between her and the door.

"I was just thinking that Melanie here..."

"Oh no," Melanie groaned aloud. "You are not going to do this. Not now." She stared at her friend, hard and with what she hoped was threatening malice.

Abby ignored the protest. "Melanie," she repeated emphatically, "is planning to audition for the Divas in a couple weeks. And I'm sure it would be a big help to have someone who knows the ropes offer a little coaching beforehand. Would you consider that a fair trade?"

Melanie glanced around at the cash register, the scarves, the jewelry display, looking for something to hurl at her friend to end this embarrassment. Instead, she hurled her words. "Honestly, you can't expect him... or me... or—"

"Hold on." Taz cocked his head to the side and stared at Melanie. "If you're serious, you'd be kind of perfect. My sister would hate you."

"Hey," Melanie cried, "you don't have to be mean."

He threw his hands up in defense. "I'm not. I mean it in the best possible way. It's just your tattoos. She can't stand them, especially on women. If I know her, she'll back off the minute she sees you. I think it might work."

"What about the coaching?" Abby piped up.

"I can't promise you a spot or anything," he said, "but I've seen what Garrett and his choreographers tend to like and not like."

Abby's face could hardly contain her grin. "What do you think, Melanie? You'll do it, right?"

Was she serious? They both seemed to think this stupid scheme could work.

Taz turned to her with a big, goofy grin. "C'mon, Melanie," he cooed. "Wanna be my pretend girlfriend?"

Why was her heart jumping inside her chest? Why did she feel like she was going to throw up? This was stupid. She shouldn't even care.

Abby sidled up to her like a car salesman on the make. "You're single now and you're going to be spending your time preparing for the audition anyway, right? Just say you'll do it. What do you have to lose?"

My integrity? My sanity?

She was not going to be Taz Roman's pretend anything. Every ounce of her screamed against this ridiculous, terrible, awful idea. "No way," she blurted. "Absolutely not." She glanced at the wall clock and slammed down the scarf she was holding in a death grip. "I've got to go."

She snatched up her purse and stormed out of the boutique, kicking aside the empty boxes in her way.

CHAPTER FOUR

ONCE MELANIE WAS cruising up Harbor Boulevard in her '68 Squareback with the window down, her elbow propped on the ledge, and rockabilly music blaring through the speakers, she felt better. Not great, but better.

She could breathe. She could think. Even with this hot wind pressing on her, smashing the barrel curl of her bangs against her forehead. She hardly noticed the swelter of the heat wave or the temperatures rising with every passing mile, taking her farther from the cooler ocean breeze and closer to the hot cauldron that was the center of Orange County.

It was still an improvement from the studio and Abby's ambush. She focused on that as she pulled into the Bella Garden Mobile Home Park, a raggedy corner of a place wedged between the 22 and 55 freeways. She rolled through the gravel lane till she saw her mother's 1970s powder-blue single-wide with the bent window screen and the sun-bleached awning hanging limp and crooked over the porch.

She crunched along the gravel until she reached the screen door and pulled it back. She paused. Should she knock? Barge in? She'd been back a week, and she still wasn't sure.

"Well, come in if you're gonna come in," a nicotine-soaked voice bellowed from inside.

She sighed. *Glad to see you, too, Mom.* She smoothed her hair and turned the knob.

Ginger Drake was in her usual place—the old brown recliner, with an ashtray and a can of cola at her elbow and that black box of a television perched on the shelves in front of her.

Melanie went to the living room curtain that had once been a cheerful lime green but was now bleached into a sickly pastel shade. She pulled it open, letting in a hard stream of late-morning sun.

"Don't do that." Her mother winced like a creature from a horror film. "It puts a glare on the TV. Close it up."

"You shouldn't sit around in the dark all day, Ma. You could grow mushrooms in this place. It's not healthy. It's a nice day outside."

"No, it's not. Too damn hot."

Melanie couldn't argue with that. It was cooler in here. That ugly window-box air conditioner rumbled like a lawn mower, but at least it worked. If only it could do something about the smell of cigarettes and disdain. She pulled the curtain halfway back over the window and settled into a chair at the dinette table that filled the tiny space dividing what her mother considered the living room and the kitchen.

She glanced at the ice pack strapped on her mother's right foot with a bandage. "Did you make a doctor's appointment yet, like I asked?"

"Oh, get off your high horse. I don't need you telling me what to do. I'm still your mother." Her eyes never veered from the flickering screen. "I'm not goin' to a doctor. They just want your money. Cut you up or put you on pills, or both. Usually both. No, thank you. I can live with bunions."

Even from this distance, Melanie could see the swelling was worse. "You have to do something, Ma. You can't just sit here."

"I get around just fine. What about you? You went to bed early then snuck out before dawn. No goodbye, no note to say where you were going or when you'd be back. This isn't a hotel, you know."

Melanie glanced around. If it were a hotel, she'd be having a word with the manager about the maid service. "I had things to do."

"Always things to do. Always too busy to spend time with your mother."

Of course. Her usual complaint. "I'm here now." She rose and went to the refrigerator, opened the freezer door, and leaned in, welcoming the cold blast. She needed to put at least a few more feet between herself and her mother. She plunged her hand into the bucket beneath the ice maker and let the chill seep into her bones.

"Get me a soda while you're in there."

"Sure." She wiped her hand on a threadbare kitchen towel hanging from the oven handle and, with her cold and stiff hand, she grabbed two of the dozens of cans crammed onto the fridge's top shelf.

Melanie walked them over to her mother and set one on the crocheted doily. She kept the other for herself.

Her mother looked up at her, the corner of her eyes pulled down. "So what was so important that you had to sneak out at the break of dawn?"

"I wasn't sneaking out, but I did want to help Abby with the studio."

Her mom grabbed the black brick of a remote and aimed it at the television screen. The channels flipped, and Melanie settled back onto the dinette chair's vinyl cushion. The television paused on something that sounded like a shopping channel, then moved on to a cooking show, and finally stopped on a home-decorating show.

"Aren't you getting too old for that stuff?" Ginger sneered. "It's a waste of time, you know. All that wiggling around for strangers. It's disgusting. Is that why your boyfriend threw you out? Your father would never have tolerated that kind of thing."

Melanie's soda can popped as she squeezed a dent into its side. "I'm not 'wiggling around,'" she said through clenched teeth. "Belly dance requires skill, just like ballet or jazz. Chet and I, we just didn't work out. I told you that."

"Right," her mom sneered. "Didn't work out, mmm-hmm. Did you even try? I doubt it. Well, I have a news flash for you, honey: you aren't getting any younger."

"Twenty-three is not exactly ancient."

"Maybe not, but you'll get there soon enough. The way you carry on with that dancing, and dressing up like you think you're some kind of '50s pin-up girl. You act like you're Bettie God-damn Page. You know, she died broke and alone. All those seam stockings and tight skirts didn't do her a bit of good in the end. Do you think they're going to do any better for you?"

"They're just clothes." Melanie stared at the condensation collecting on her glass. Like a hundred tiny tears fighting the urge to fall. "It's just a dance." She pulled her phone from her purse and checked the time. Had it only been ten minutes? It felt like an hour. If her mother opened her mouth one more time... She jumped up from the table. "I'm sweaty from the drive. I'm gonna take a shower."

"Do what you want," her mother said, never taking her eyes off the screen. "You always do anyway."

Melanie turned on the water the instant she entered the cramped bathroom, with its pink porcelain sink and matching toilet. Her mom thought the silver foil wallpaper with fuzzy pink flowers "opened up the room." Melanie had thought it looked sad and desperate when her mother put it up ten years ago, when they'd moved into the place after Dad left. And it looked even worse now, with its peeling and ripped edges and the water stain in the corner. She stared into the mirror as the steam accumulated around her.

Why had she come back here? When Abby offered up her couch, she should have taken it. She shouldn't have let her pride get in the way. A little shame seemed like a small price to pay compared to this churning, aching feeling in her gut. All the guilt, regret, and pain she felt every time she stood under this roof.

She tried to shake the feeling by peeling off her black yoga pants and the black shredded tee-shirt over the cherry red tank. Other people's parents softened as they got older. Not Ginger. Every year she just got crankier and more withdrawn.

When every thread of clothing sat in a pile on the floor and the air dripped with moist, heavy heat, she stepped into the narrow, pink stall. She flinched when the spray hit her like a thousand burning needles. Slowly, oh so slowly, she relaxed into the sensation. The pain seared everything else away: every thought, every worry, every regret. When the water was hot enough, it numbed her to everything else.

She let it wash away the perspiration from the drive, and let it rinse away her exhaustion even as it turned her skin an angry shade of pink.

She stayed there, wrapped in the water's hot embrace, until the heat became part of her, until her flesh burned red, until even the hottest setting no longer had any effect. She turned off the water, wrapped a frayed towel around her, and tried to find her way back to the ordinary world.

She wiped the fog from the mirror and hardly recognized the face in front of her. No mascara, no eyeliner, no lipstick. Not to mention all the kink and frizz in her hair. All the work from her morning date with her curling iron and the flat iron completely down the drain. She pulled the damp mass back into a ponytail and tried to brush it into a curl. She gave up. It wasn't like her mother would tear herself away from the television long enough to notice anyway.

She was wrong.

"You look like a drowned rat," Ginger said when she returned to the front room after grabbing herself another soda.

When Melanie didn't answer, Ginger poked again. "If you paraded around like that at Chet's place, it's no wonder he kicked you out."

Melanie closed her eyes. She wished she was someplace else.

Her mother smirked. "If you knew how to treat a man, you wouldn't be in this mess."

Melanie's hands balled into fists. She knew she should keep quiet. Anything she said would only egg her mother on. The words came flying out anyway. "What mess exactly? My life is just fine, thank you. If you want to know the truth, I left Chet. I dumped him, Ma. No one ever dumps me."

Her mother's eyes snapped in her direction. Her lip curled with disgust. "I suppose you're proud of yourself then. You're too good to be dumped, is that it? Not like your mother. She's just worthless, right? A doormat a man can wipe his feet on before walking away."

"Don't," Melanie said, the word clawing through her. "We don't have to fight about this. Chet and I didn't work out. End of story."

Her mother folded her arms over her house dress. "So you think I'm going to say, 'Oh, it's all right.' Well, guess what, Peaches. It isn't going to be all right. When are you going to grow up and realize you're damn lucky if a man is willing to put up with your shit? But, no, you're much better at pushing men away, aren't you? You pushed your father away and you've been pushing away any man who looks at you twice ever since."

Melanie shot up from her chair, tipping the half-filled can and spilling fizzy soda across the linoleum floor. She looked at it, but she didn't move to clean it up. She grabbed her clutch and her keys instead. "It's been great spending time with you, Ma. I gotta go."

Her mother sat up straight. "Don't walk out when I'm talking to you, Melanie Jean. You get back in here."

But Melanie was already out the door and down the steps. Her hand was on the hot chrome door handle when she heard it. Her mother's usual parting comment: "You're worthless, you know. Absolutely worthless."

Melanie dropped into the seat behind the steering wheel, cranked the ignition, and drove.

She drove down Harbor and down Newport Boulevard. Halfway between Newport Beach and Laguna on Coast Highway, she pulled into the cliff-side Shake Shack with her mother's words still rattling in her head. Ginger was bitter. She was vengeful. At this point, she might even be psychotic.

But she also had a point.

What did Melanie have that was worth anything? A clerical job she tolerated. A crappy car. A string of ex-boyfriends.

Dancing. That was all she really had. The only thing she cared about, anyway. Feeling herself in the music, feeling part of it, feeling it move through her. It didn't matter that she couldn't afford college and certainly never had the grades to get a scholarship. It didn't matter that she didn't have family connections to land a great job after squeaking through high school. What she had was dance, and somehow that was going to be her ticket to something better. She'd always known it. She talked about it. She expected it.

It was no wonder Abby assumed she was going to try out for the Belly Dance Divas. Everyone assumed it. It wasn't that she'd decided against it. She just hadn't gotten around to the paperwork yet. There was still plenty of time for that. Plenty of time to put these nagging doubts to rest.

But then Abby had tried to force her into that arrangement with Taz.

She made it sound so simple. So easy. Like it was a sure thing. She'd never understand that if Melanie lost this dream, she'd have nothing.

She couldn't bear that.

But now it hardly mattered. She'd made a mess of everything. A mediocre job, a mediocre car, and let's face it, a worse than mediocre life. Without even trying, she was sinking into the same abyss that had claimed her mother. In twenty years, she would be her mother, hating the world and everyone in it because she'd never had a chance for something better.

Only, she did have a chance. Taz Roman was offering to help her get into the Divas. How could she turn that down?

She couldn't. Even if she was scared. Even if it all came to nothing. She had to try.

She grabbed her phone before she lost her nerve and dialed.

"Abby, it's me. Do you have Taz's number?"

There was stunned silence for a fat second, then, "I can do better than that. He's right here."

Melanie's heart raced. Her cheeks flushed. Damn, why couldn't she just leave this on his voicemail?

"Hey, this is Taz."

She took a quick, deep breath. "It's Melanie," she said and clenched her fists, her eyes, her everything. "Is that offer still open?"

CHAPTER FIVE

MELANIE STARED OVER her steering wheel into the tangerine glow sliding over the Pacific. The clear silhouette of Catalina Island was in the distance. "If I'm going to do this, there have to be some ground rules."

A pause stretched on the other end of the line, then Taz replied, "What'd you have in mind?"

"For starters," she said, "I want to know exactly what I get in this bargain."

"Fair enough. Let's talk over dinner. I'm playing at the Tent tonight."

The Sultan's Tent was a Middle Eastern restaurant and nightclub in Newport Beach that attracted the local rich and trendy crowd. Over-hyped and overpriced, it was also the most coveted job around for belly dancers and like-minded musicians. Abby had worked there until the studio's business turned around. Melanie hoped she would too, someday.

"I could pick you up, we could have a drink, maybe some dinner, and discuss it."

His voice dripped with effortless charm. She had to remind herself this was Taz. This is what he did.

"Sure," she said. "I just have to check on one thing. Just give me a minute..." She fumbled for her purse and pulled out her wallet. The Tent could be great for tips, but it was pretty hard on the budget.

"My treat," he said, dangling the words like carrots.

She closed her eyes, embarrassed. Had she been so obvious? "Just checking my calendar. Yeah, I'm open."

"Great. What time should I pick you up?"

That could be a problem. Quickly, she recalibrated. "How about I meet you there?"

"All right."

"Seven?" she added quickly.

"Abby was right about you," he said. "Once you put your mind to something..." He didn't finish the thought, and she didn't want to ask.

"So seven works?" she pressed again.

"Seven works."

CHAPTER SIX

A FEW HOURS later, after another difficult exchange with her mother, Melanie pulled into the Tent's parking lot. The sun hung low on the horizon, casting long shadows across the highway and giving the multi-million-dollar homes perched on the cliffs a bright, fiery glow. She took the last gulp of her diet soda, dropped the can in the cup holder, and maneuvered up to the obligatory valet station, trying not to notice the rows of luxury cars beyond. A silver Bentley, a black Ferrari, that distinctive yellow coupe.

A teen with a mop of blue-streaked hair jogged up to her door. She hopped out and noticed him glancing at the dingy windows and the dented side panel. She dropped the key in his palm. "Sorry, Skippy. We don't all drive Porsches. Get over it."

He smirked and mumbled, "Enjoy your evening, ma'am." He emphasized the last word, aiming it like a dart at her vanity. It stung, but not as much as his dollar tip would later.

She wrapped her newly painted fingertips around a red clutch and steered her black stilettos to the door with her head high, ready to take on the world. Or at least Taz Roman.

Look, there he was, all hair and teeth and shoulders. His *doumbek* hooked under one of those giant arms, an Egyptian pyramid on the horizon behind him. The poster hanging at the door made her groan. What a pretty boy. Definitely not her type. Then again, maybe that was going to make this whole thing easier. Let him play his playboy tricks. She was immune.

Inside, she could hear the music pounding, a blend of traditional Middle Eastern rhythms and modern techno-rock. There was a distinct emphasis on the drumming that had to be Taz. She took a deep breath, inhaling the roasted meats and savory Moroccan dishes the Tent was known for, and steeled herself before pulling open the door to find the restaurant's foyer filled to capacity with waiting bodies.

Great. She'd have a nice, long wait before she got the opportunity to demean herself. Maybe that wasn't such a bad thing. A twinge in her belly reminded her of the soda she'd guzzled getting ready and the other one she'd downed while driving. At least there'd be time for a trip to the ladies' room.

The door opened again behind her, and a large, laughing party entered. Three or four couples? She edged up to the hostess stand. No need to make the wait any longer than it had to be. She leaned over the counter to be heard above the chaos of chatter and music. "I don't have a reservation, but I'm supposed to meet with the guy who's performing tonight." She knew it sounded ridiculous the moment she said it. Before she could rephrase, the head of a blond, bright-eyed hostess popped up.

"Oh," chirped the woman. "You must be Melanie. Taz's friend?"

Melanie straightened. Friend? "Yeah, I guess that's me." She hid her surprise behind a frozen smile.

"Come with me, we have a table for you." The hostess grabbed a menu and pushed through the crowd.

Melanie glanced around at the others still waiting. More than one glowered in her direction. She shrugged her apology, turned and hurried after the hostess.

The dining room was nearly as packed as the foyer, but all eyes were on the stage, where Taz sat in the center with a full band at his back: traditional instruments like an *oud*, *mizmar*, and *ney*, playing alongside an electric keyboard and something that looked like an electric sitar.

The hostess stopped at a two-seat table beside the stage and plucked off a "reserved" sign. Melanie settled into the seat with a perfect view of the stage.

The hostess leaned down to her ear. "Your waiter will be with you in a moment, but I can get you something from the bar, if you'd like."

Something about the way she hesitated made the girl quickly add: "Don't worry. It's on the house."

Melanie would have been embarrassed if she weren't so relieved. "A dirty martini, please. Three olives, if you can."

"Three olives, no problem." The girl was gone, swallowed by the crowd.

When Melanie glanced up, Taz was staring back at her. Again, those startling green eyes seemed to penetrate her. He winked.

That inconvenient twinge returned. She crossed her legs, forced a smile, and waved, wishing she had opted for the ladies' room when she had the chance.

At the end of the song, he pulled the microphone from his drum to his lips. "Thank you for the warm welcome. It's always a pleasure to be back at the Tent."

The applause drowned his next words. He paused. When it had quieted, he leaned into the mic again. "A friend of mine is in the audience tonight. A terrific dancer I know you would love to meet. Would you like to meet her?"

The crowd clapped and whooped. Someone in a back corner whistled. Melanie glanced around. Who was it? Someone from the Divas? Someone she knew?

"Melanie Drake, how about joining me on the stage?"

She whipped around. He locked gazes with her and smiled in a way that didn't quite reach his eyes.

She froze. Was he serious? She was in a wiggle skirt and pumps, for crying out loud. And, damn, she really needed a ladies' room.

She glanced around at the crowd that was still whooping and clapping. Every eye in the place seemed to be turned her way. Her stomach fell to her feet.

She dropped her glance to the floor and shook her head. A demure but polite refusal. No way was she going up there. No frigging way.

But Taz didn't let up. He rose and made his way to the edge of the stage. "She must be feeling shy tonight. How about we coax her a little?" He joined in the clapping. A few more whistles joined the chorus. At her shoulder, a nice-looking woman smiled and whispered, "C'mon, it'll be fun."

Fun. Yeah, like a root canal.

But one thing she knew: when things get out of control, it's best to drive into the skid. It's the only way to survive. She took a breath and stood. The applause ratcheted up. She locked gazes with Taz again and gave him a long, you'll-pay-for-this look as she made her way past the densely packed tables and chairs between her and the stage. Taz met her at the short stack of stairs on the side, took her hand, and led her to the center of the stage, as though he were a gentleman and not the devil incarnate.

"I'm gonna kill you for this," she muttered between her clenched-teeth smile.

"You'll be fine," he whispered back. She offered a weak smile to the six-pack band behind him, who were either smiling at her or laughing at her. Maybe both.

Taz grabbed his microphone again. "Here's what we're going to do. We're going to improvise a little. I'll start playing. You and the band can join in when you feel comfortable. Ready?" He glanced back. The musicians nodded and gave him a thumbs up. He looked at her.

She wanted to flip him off and run to the nearest exit. Maybe he thought this was funny. Humiliate her in front of all these people. Show her she wasn't ready to dance in the big time. Put her in her place. Well, she wasn't going to give him the satisfaction.

She sauntered back to the staircase, listening to the audience gasps. They expected her to flee. She looked out over the faces staring up at her, glowing pink and blue in the darkness from the stage lights. She turned up a coy smile, winked, and kicked off her stilettos. Then she walked along the stage's edge, searching... searching... perfect! She pointed to a woman wrapped in a white silky shawl with long floss fringe. "May I borrow your wrap?"

The woman brightened, unwound it from her neck, and offered it up. Melanie thanked her and tied it around her hips. When it was secure, she shimmied and the crowd oohed and ahhed.

Behind her, Taz said, "Well, folks. I'd say she's ready. What about you?"

The crowd cheered.

With a plastered, false smile, she sauntered back to where he had pulled his drum up onto his thigh and gave him a smirk she hoped said, "I can take whatever you dish out, pretty boy."

He launched into a *taksim*, a slow melody with a strong, slithering beat.

Her hips twitched to the rhythm, and then smoothed the move into a graceful sway. The music sank deeper beneath her skin and the movement rose from her hips to her chest. Her body wove endless circles and figure eights. She focused her attention on Taz, which was all she could do because the spotlight blinded her to anything else. She studied his fingers on the drum skin, and soon it was as though she could anticipate his notes. If he changed the rhythm, she was right there with him. If he paused, she stopped on cue. Even the incessant and uncomfortable twinge had disappeared.

Wrapped in the spotlight, it was as if no one else existed. Just the two of them, playing and teasing. She followed his lead, then he seemed to follow hers. It was so easy, this back and forth. It was even fun.

Maybe he wasn't so bad after all.

But then, just as quickly as it had begun, it all stopped. The music. The glances. Everything. He set his drum on the floor and stood, took her hand, and led her in a quick bow to the audience. He kept her hand in his through the surging applause, but then all but pushed her back toward the stairs.

Confusion then anger burned through her. Was this some kind of power trip? Whatever it was, she didn't like it. And she certainly didn't like him. He might get away with that kind of thing with other women, but not her. All the good looks in the world didn't earn him the right to humiliate her like that. To think she thought this whole stupid scheme might work. She should have listened to her gut.

She tossed the scarf back to its owner, scooped up her shoes, and descended the stage stairs. At her lonely table, she snatched up her clutch and marched past the martini now waiting for her. She ignored the smiles and pats on the back from the strangers in her path. With a brittle smile, she pushed through all of it with one driving goal: to leave. She was no marionette for Taz Roman to control. She hated him. She never wanted to see him again. She wanted to get home, crawl into bed, and never come out.

But damn, her bladder was about to explode. She'd never make it home. She probably wouldn't make it to her car. She clenched her thigh muscles as she pressed on. It was no use. One stop in the ladies' room, then she'd leave.

CHAPTER SEVEN

THE TENT'S EMPTY ladies' room looked like something the *Lawrence of Arabia* set designer would dream up, with decorative wall tiles and sumptuous burgundy drapes, but it was just a blur to Melanie as she rushed in and found an empty stall.

She peeled the snug black skirt over her thighs and dropped onto the cool wooden seat. Finally, relief.

The restroom door opened while she sat, and then she wasn't alone anymore.

"No way, that was part of the act," said a woman with a drawl thicker than Texas toast.

Another one answered in a timid, mouse-like voice. "Maybe, but it looked improvised to me. Kinda like they knew each other. But I'm sure you're right. You know him better than I do."

Melanie tried to peek beneath the stall but could see only two sets of wedge sandals making their way into stalls on the other side of the room.

When both women were behind locked doors, Melanie flushed and yanked up her skirt. She had to get out before either of them saw her. She didn't need more embarrassment heaped onto the rest. She bee-lined it to the sinks and soaked her hands quickly, grabbed a paper towel, and dried her hands.

"Of course I'm right," the Southern one said. "You can't just improvise something that good."

Melanie froze with the paper towel in her hand. They were talking about her. They thought she was *good*.

"Wait," the Southern one added, "what do you mean it looked like they knew each other?"

"I don't know," the timid one said. "Didn't it seem like there was something between them? Some kind of chemistry?"

Chemistry? What did that mean? Melanie waited to hear more, but the women were finishing up. She heard a toilet flush. Damn! She should leave, but she wanted to know what that woman meant. The stall door pulled open.

Melanie lunged back into her empty stall and slammed it closed. She sat and wrapped her arms around herself, and tried to calm her thumping heart.

The women didn't pay any attention. Melanie could see them both at the sink through the sliver of space between the door and the post.

"I'll bet she was one of the Belly Dance Divas," said the Southern one, pulling a pocket-sized brush through her wild mass of blond hair.

"I don't think so," the other one said, hardly glancing at her own thin, brown bob. "I didn't recognize her."

"It'll come to me," the blonde said, stuffing the brush back into her purse.

"If she is with him, are you still going to talk to him?"

The purse dropped with a thud on the counter. "Why would you even ask me that? Of course I am. It's just an interview." She stopped. "That's how I remember her. I interviewed her for the blog when the Divas performed at the Lava Theatre last year. She's not a soloist, but in the company. Absolutely."

"I still can't believe I missed that show," the brunette said. "I begged for the night off, and I was still scheduled to work."

"You better make sure it doesn't happen next weekend. Do you know how hard it was to get those Pandemonium Ball tickets?"

The conversation wandered away from Melanie and the Belly Dance Divas, and on to the more practical matter of managing a frustrating work supervisor. Melanie stopped listening. She was still stuck on the earlier comment about her.

They thought she was a Diva. Really?

Maybe she had a better chance at the audition than she thought.

But if she did, she better not blow it by walking out on Taz Roman.

CHAPTER EIGHT

"OH, MR. ROMAN, that was so amazing. I hope I'm not bothering you."

Taz snapped his drum in its case. "Nope. What can I do for you?" His answer was crisp, bordering on curt, and he didn't turn around as he propped his instrument at the edge of the stage. It wasn't his usual way of dealing with after-show fans. His father had taught him better than that.

"When you perform, you belong to the audience," Leopold Roman would say in that accent that was as thick as the Carpathian forests until the day he died. "Before the show, during the show, and after. That is the performer's life, Tazarian."

Taz had taken the words to heart. Ordinarily, he'd drop anything to chat, and it didn't hurt that most of the time the fans seeking his attention were sweet, starstruck women with kitten-soft voices that did dangerous things to his thoughts. Just as this one would've been doing if he could just shake the feeling that he'd made a terrible mistake, or silence that little voice in his head telling him it wasn't too late.

Go after her.

"I was just hoping you might autograph this for me," the woman cooed.

He turned, and it was just as he'd suspected. She was a petite platinum blonde with a dress cut low to reveal her perfectly tanned, perfectly plump assets, and legs—he dipped a quick glance—oh man, legs that were tailor-made for those red-hot stilettos.

Those legs alone might have brought him back to his senses if he could just take his eyes off the door and get rid of the gnawing in his gut.

Why had he pushed Melanie? Why hadn't he stuck to his plan? Put her on the spot for a moment and see how she handled herself. See if there was anything there.

He'd expected a shoulder shimmy or two. Maybe a playful undulation. What she'd given him would have knocked him on his ass if he weren't already sitting down. The woman had moves—that was obvious. Not to mention a body with all the right curves, even without one of those glitzy stage costumes that could make a tree branch look good.

But it was more than that. She had connected with the music in a way he'd never experienced before. It was as if she anticipated him, or maybe it was the other way around. Damn, it had all happened so fast, and as soon as he realized what was happening, he'd shut it down. He wasn't even sure why.

Go after her.

But one hopeful, upturned gaze stopped him. That promise he made to his father at least a hundred times.

That is the life, Tazarian.

With a frustrated sigh that he hoped his smile would disguise, he took the sliver of paper the woman was handing to him along with a pen. "Absolutely. What's your name, darlin'?"

She giggled. "Charlotte. Charlotte Beaudreaux. Would you mind if my husband and I sit with you during the break?"

CHAPTER NINE

WHEN MELANIE RETURNED to the dining room, she had a fresh layer of lipstick, freshly brushed hair, and a fresh attitude. She walked in to find the stage cleared and the crowd thinned. Taz was sitting at her table with a beer bottle in his hand, holding court with the nearby diners like he was some kind of king. The way he flashed his white, perfectly straight teeth and tossed his loose hair back over his shoulder, he didn't seem to have a care in the world.

It made her resent him just a little bit more.

Did he expect her to grovel to get his help? Her instincts told her again to turn around and march out the door.

It wasn't like her instincts had been much help lately. If she didn't give this a try, she'd regret it forever, even if she didn't make the Divas.

She had killed it up there. She knew it. Even those women in the ladies' room knew it. She had a chance, probably her best one ever.

If Taz wanted to make it difficult, fine. Let him. She could deal with it. Besides, she had an advantage when it came to him: she was immune to that million-dollar smile of his. If he wanted to play games, let him. Bring it on.

She turned on her own million-dollar smile—or what she hoped passed for one—and walked up to the table as if she were expected.

He turned up a wide grin. "There you are. I thought you'd abandoned me."

Was that real surprise or sarcasm? She tried reading between the laugh lines tugging at the corners of his eyes. He was still soaking in the adoration. Still on. Maybe he never turned it off.

Then he stood and pulled out her chair. So, the big gorilla at least had some manners. "Thank you," she said tightly.

The blonde who had urged her on before turned a big, fuchsia smile at her. "Your ears must have been burning. We were just talking about you."

Melanie faked a smile. "Oh?"

"Nothing bad, of course." The woman batted her hand playfully. "We were just saying how wonderful you were up there. Both of you, really. You must perform together a lot."

"No, actually," Melanie said, trying to detect whether the woman was putting her on. "It was a first, and I hope the last."

"Don't say that," the woman cried a little too effusively. Her words slurred just a bit. "You could feel all that chemistry up there. It was very sexy—"

"Charlotte, honey," the man in the suit sitting beside her reached out and touched her shoulder. "I'm not sure that's appropriate."

The woman turned a wide, confused gaze at him. "What do you mean? I only meant they're a cute couple." She turned back to Melanie and Taz. "Right? I didn't offend you, did I?"

The man stood and gathered her up with an apologetic look. "C'mon, Charlotte, we shouldn't monopolize Mr. Roman's time."

"Oh, you're no fun. All right. Well, Mr. Roman, it sure has been a pleasure talking with you and your friend."

Melanie noticed the way the woman leaned forward when she offered her hand. It was hard to say whether she meant to call attention to the plumpness peeking between the deep V of her clingy wrap dress, but Taz certainly seemed to notice it.

"The pleasure was all mine," he said, staring directly at her breasts.

As the man pulled the woman toward the door, Melanie introduced herself to the martini with three olives awaiting her.

Taz watched the couple leave, then slanted a look her direction. "I didn't think you were coming back."

She feigned surprise. "Why? You don't think I enjoy being put on the spot like that? No warning? No preparation? It keeps life so interesting."

Her sarcasm sparked amusement in his expression. "You can't blame me, can you?"

"Excuse me?" Was he really that cruel?

He shrugged. "I need to know what I have to work with before I agree to anything. That's just good business."

"Business?" She leaned against the chair's backrest, stunned—and still furious. "That was your idea of a fun little test, then?"

He glanced away, considering it, then nodded. "Yeah, if you want to call it that. Look, I know you can dance on your home turf, in front of a friendly crowd. I've heard that much. But performing on big stages in strange cities where nobody knows you, that's not the same thing. I need to know how you do under pressure."

She set down her martini glass, and a splash of gin sloshed over the rim. "You asked around about me? Why? When?" The questions were racing through her brain faster than she could spit them out.

"Today. After you left the studio."

"But I told you I wasn't interested. I told you no."

"I had a feeling you'd come around."

Melanie replayed the scene. There was no way. She'd been clear when she left. She cocked her chin. "It was Abby, wasn't it? What did she tell you?"

His glance skittered away again. "Nothing I didn't already know."

She folded her arms and planted her elbows on the table. "What do you think you know about me?"

He fixed her with a steel glare. "I don't even have to know you to know you," he said. His jaw tensed as he stared, not at her, but through her, into her past, into her secrets.

She shifted, but he didn't ease up.

"I see your kind all the time," he said. "You want to be a Belly Dance Diva. You want it so bad you can taste it. You can smell it. But you let your nerves get the better of you. You're a good dancer, maybe even great, but when the pressure turns up, you fall apart. You want it, but you're afraid of it. How am I doing so far?"

Hitting the nail on the head, but she'd never give him the satisfaction of telling him that. "I want it," she shot back. "I'll give you that. But I'm not afraid to fail."

"Then why haven't you ever tried out before? Auditions happen every year, and I've never seen you there."

"I've been busy. I have a job. Besides, my boyfriend wasn't exactly excited about the idea of me being off on tour for months at a time."

His eyes flashed. "A boyfriend? How'd you change his mind?"

"I didn't. That's why he's an ex-boyfriend," she said, shredding the corner of her cocktail napkin into bits. "My point is that I'm ready, and I want this, and I can do it without your help. I'm just smart enough to know that when an opportunity comes up, you take it." Her gaze slid across the tabletop and climbed up slowly to meet his. "So let's not forget who really needs who here."

He tipped back his beer bottle and smiled, like she'd just passed another secret test. She resisted the urge to reach over and slap that smug look off his face.

He set down his bottle with a thump. "Okay. Here's what I'm *not* going to do," he said. "I'm not going to guarantee you a spot in the troupe. I couldn't even if I wanted to. The producer makes those decisions. I sit on the audition panel, along with the choreographer and a few others, but Garrett makes the final call. He has the vision. You're going to have to earn it the same way everybody else earns it."

She opened her mouth to reply, but he stopped her with a raised finger.

"But," he continued, "in the years I've been working with him, I've sat through a lot of auditions and rehearsals, and I know what he's looking for. I know what he likes, and more important, I know what he doesn't."

The way he was staring at her made her shift uneasily in her seat. "If you have something to say, just say it."

He shrugged. "I just want you to know that all I can offer is advice. I'll critique your routine. I will give you pointers, but I cannot and will not promise you a spot. If you think that's worth your time, then we'll talk about my part of the bargain."

Melanie took another sip—a gulp, really—of her martini. She felt the alcohol burn its way down her throat and warm her belly. Was it worth it? She broke off their standoff stare. Her gaze brushed over the silky, white sheers along the windows, billowing gently from the breeze coming in off Newport Bay. He wasn't offering her a sure thing, far from it. But it was still an edge. "Yeah, I'm in. What do I have to do?"

He leaned back, looking relieved. "For starters, you'll have to move in with me."

She sputtered the martini that was at her lips. She set the glass down. "Are you kidding me? Why?"

His overabundance of confidence vanished. "I know. It's a lot. But I kinda mentioned that to my sister, that you and I—well, my girlfriend and I—were living together."

"When you decide to lie, you really go all out. Honestly, I've never been happier to be an only child."

"I know. It was a stupid thing to do. She wanted to stay at the house..." He stopped, shook his head, and tried again. "I thought if I told her she couldn't, she wouldn't come. She hates hotels. Obviously, my plan backfired. So I need a live-in girlfriend. That's number one."

Okay, she hadn't expected that, but it wasn't a deal breaker. "What else?"

He shrugged. "I don't know. I guess you have to act like you don't hate me."

She tilted her head. "You think I hate you?"

His eyes widened. "Seriously? You make it pretty obvious. So I'm just saying—you know—pretend when she's around, if you can."

If you can?

Behind her, she heard a shuffling and a distant but unmistakable voice whisper, "Just do it. Just ask him."

She didn't turn to look who had said it, and she didn't let it distract her. Instead, she reached over and laid her palm on the soft bed of sandy curls on his forearm. When his muscles tensed, her lips stretched into a slow, seductive smile. She made a sad Snoopy face. "You don't really think I hate you, do you?"

His glance flashed to something behind her, but only for a moment, and then his attention was again riveted on her. Beneath her hand, his muscles eased. Not just where she touched him, but the shifting in his seat told her the effect was moving south, too.

"I don't know. Maybe."

She made a soft *tsk-tsk-tsk* sound. "Now what if I told you that I do like you, Taz Roman. I like you very much."

He pulled back and threw his other arm over the chair's back, angling his body to give her a better view of his partially exposed chest. "When you put it like that, I guess I was wrong. You just always seem annoyed by me, I guess. Irritated."

Was that a tinge of pink around his neck? It was almost endearing. But she wasn't ready to let up. Not yet.

She lowered her voice to a whisper. "A girl has to keep a guy guessing, doesn't she? She has to have some mystery to keep his interest."

His chest was rising and falling with quickening breaths. "Yeah, I get that," he said.

She stretched back slowly against her chair with that sexy, seductive smile and then dropped it like a hot coal. "Good. Because if you believe it, I'm sure your sister will, too."

His smile vanished. "Wait, that was fake? You were faking all that?"

She wiggled her eyebrows. "I'm good, huh? You aren't the only one who can lie."

He frowned and rose from his seat. "Okay, you proved your point. I think I need another drink. Can I get you something?"

She shook her head. "No, I'm good."

As he walked toward the bar, she heard him mutter, "Maybe too good."

When he was gone, she exhaled the breath she didn't realize she'd been holding. She watched him saunter back to the bar, and looked around. Who had been trying to get their attention? Then she saw the shroud of blond hair marching out the dining room door, followed closely by a short, brunette bob, and she knew. The bloggers from the ladies' room. Apparently she'd gotten in the middle of their exclusive interview.

Should she feel bad? Probably. But the last thing he needed was more adoring fans, and she needed to prove her point.

She had, but she'd gotten something else, too. She stared at her fingers. It was back. The hot tingle that had pulsed through her like a licking flame when she touched him. She curled her hands into fists, trying to force the feeling back, and trying to get herself back under control.

A few minutes later, he slid with effortless grace back into his chair.

"I guess there's just one more thing to discuss," he said and took a slow sip of what looked like a shot of whiskey.

She clamped her hands together and held them in her lap, far from him, and far from danger. "What now?" she asked, laying on the snark. "Personal references? Work history?"

"Nope." He smirked. "Just a question. How soon can you move in?"

CHAPTER TEN

FOUR DAYS LATER, Melanie stood in front of a ten-foot-tall river rock wall with a suitcase on wheels beside her. She punched the buzzer on the security system and saw her own black-and-white image flicker to life on the closed-circuit television screen perched above her. Damn, this place was a fortress. When Taz had given her his address, she had expected the Huntington Beach neighborhood to be nice and probably near the water. She didn't expect it to be one of the waterfront mansions in the priciest part of the harbor. These secluded homes were the kinds of places where you expected to find movie stars or sports heroes, not *doumbek* drummers.

"You're late," a familiar voice growled through the speaker.

"I hit traffic. I'm surprised I got here at all."

"You should have taken side streets."

"I'll make a note," she snapped back. She wasn't going to mention that traffic wasn't the only cause of her delay. When she'd planned how long it would take to pack, she hadn't factored in the extra hour to argue with her mother, who had apparently decided to take Melanie's departure as yet another personal affront.

A buzz signaled her to open the gate. She pushed the door and nearly choked at the sight of the house on the other side.

Taz stood in an arched doorway, wiping his hands with a dish towel.

"Welcome home," he said with a wry grin.

"Yeah," she muttered, her eyes still roaming over the courtyard that hugged the building's wave-like contours. Every gently curved wall was open glass, displaying an immaculately white interior and making it seem more like an aquarium than a home. In the distance, she could hear the ocean crashing against the shore and seagulls squawking at the setting sun. "You live here?"

"It's a little much, isn't it?" he said with a chuckle. "Blame my dad. He loved architecture, especially mid-century modern design. Of course, when he bought the land and commissioned the house in the '60s, people weren't calling it that. Back then, it was just modern. Now? Well, you get used to it. C'mon, I'll show you around."

He threw the towel over his shoulder, and without a word, grabbed her suitcase and wheeled it inside.

Ordinarily, she would have protested. She didn't go for that macho sense of chivalry, but she was too busy gawking at the house. It really was amazing. Like a giant, white palace. Not just the walls, but everything was white: the tiled floors, the carpets, the furniture. Only a few massive oil paintings hanging in strategic places throughout the home splashed various shades of blue. The floor-to-ceiling windows let in the colors of the ocean and the sky.

The house really was remarkable, like something a Kardashian or a Clooney might live in up in the Hollywood Hills or tucked away in Malibu. She'd always heard the Romans were considered royalty in Middle Eastern music circles. Maybe that was a lot more lucrative than she'd thought.

"This is quite a place," she said, following him deeper inside.

He glanced around at the curved staircase, recessed alcoves, and the wide open gulf designed down the middle of the house, which rose three stories to a giant skylight above. "Yeah, it's nice. My parents had a blast working with the architect. My dad especially, because he was such an architecture enthusiast. He used to take us to places like the Ennis House and Wayfarers Chapel the way other parents took their kids to Knott's Berry Farm and Disneyland. You know, before the accident."

The drop in his tone made it clear that wasn't something he wanted to discuss. She went a different direction. "So you've lived here since you were a kid?"

It didn't seem possible. Everything looked so clean, so frigging brand new.

"Only part time until a few years ago. When my parents died, my sister and I moved to Brooklyn to live with an aunt. She brought us here a couple weeks in the summer, but most of the time the place was empty. It was kept in a trust until I was eighteen and Gina was twenty."

"So you both own it, but only you live in it?"

"Yeah, for now. The will prevents us from selling until I'm thirty. That's probably another reason she wants to come back and check on me. Make sure I haven't damaged her investment."

"I can't believe you live here all alone." She wasn't going to say it, but she'd never had more than a bedroom to call her own. Lately, she didn't even have that.

"I don't live alone anymore. Now you're here." He didn't exactly sound pleased.

"Right," she said. "That's going to take some getting used to. Sorry if this is too blunt, but how in the world do you keep this place so clean? I've never met a guy who could keep a room clean, let alone a whole house, especially a house like this."

"Anna," he said.

"Huh?"

"My housekeeper. She's here Tuesdays and Fridays, unless I need her more often."

"I should have known," Melanie said. "Of course you'd have a housekeeper. That's what rich people do, right?" Inside she winced. She hadn't meant to sound snide.

If he'd been offended, he didn't show it as he parked her suitcase at the base of the stairs. He turned back with his usual cavalier smile. "I guess it's a good idea we're getting started a few days before Gina gets here. It'll give you a chance to get all your clever put-downs out of the way."

His smile never faltered, but hers vanished.

"I'm sorry. I'm just not used to this."

He held up his hand. "Don't worry about it," he said. "I know this is a weird situation. Honestly, I'm just glad you're willing to do it. Do you want to see the upstairs?"

"Do I? Absolutely." She had to admit, she was more than a little curious what her room looked like.

He lowered the telescoping handle on the suitcase and hoisted it up. "Damn," he said. "Did you pack bricks?"

She tilted her head. "Hey, you don't get to complain about my stuff. Got it?"

"Fine," he said. "But holy mackerel."

She followed him until he stopped at a bright and beautifully appointed bedroom with a view of the harbor.

"You can use this room, if you want," he said. It seemed like he had something else to say, but he gnawed his lip instead, and his fingers were tapping a nervous rhythm on her suitcase handle.

"What is it?" she asked. "Already freaked out at the thought of cohabitation?"

He shook off his awkward distraction and grinned. "Yeah, I guess. Something like that. Hey, why don't you settle in and then meet me down in the kitchen. I was just about to have dinner. You're welcome to join me."

"Really?" She couldn't remember the last time a guy offered to cook for her, but what happened to the upstairs tour? How much more incredible was this house of his? She wanted to see what was behind all these closed doors, but she couldn't muster the courage to ask. Besides, there'd be plenty of time to be nosy. "Sure, I'm starving," she said, and it wasn't a lie. "What's on the menu?"

"Soup and grilled cheese sandwiches."

She chuckled. "You really are a true-blue bachelor, aren't you?"

"Oh, you'd be surprised," he said.

"I'm sorry. I'm not trying to make fun of you," she said quickly. "Cooking isn't exactly my strong suit, either. I live on microwave meals."

"Really?"

She couldn't tell if he was agreeing with her or mocking her, so she ignored it. Instead, she grabbed her suitcase handle and wheeled it to the bed. "I can put this stuff away later. Now where's that dinner you mentioned?"

She followed him to the kitchen, where she propped herself up on his stainless-steel kitchen counter. She slid back to the floor when he gave her an odd look, like maybe she was raised in a barn. Geez, he was fussy. Was this how it was going to be?

She focused on the kitchen. The place was spotless, just like the rest of the house. All stark white and metal. It looked more like a hospital than any kitchen she'd ever been in. Who would've guessed Taz Roman was a neat freak?

She felt stiff and out of place, but he, on the other hand, couldn't have looked more comfortable. He went to work pulling packages from a refrigerator that was big enough to house a small family. From a hidden compartment atop the counter, he pulled a thick and crusty loaf of bread and cut four thick slices. From the packages, he pulled at least three different cheeses—two white and one cheddar—and cut slices from them as well. He poured a container of a reddish-orange puree soup into a pot and turned up one of the industrial-sized burners.

She watched, fascinated. When he was watching the sandwiches on the griddle, she asked something she'd wanted to ask the moment she arrived. "So, uh, how long is your sister going to be here?" *And more importantly, how long do I have to be here?*

"She didn't say exactly," he said, shaking the grill pan slightly.

Her attention was drawn to a stack of Pandemonium Ball fliers on the counter, just like the ones he'd left with Abby. She took one. The fantasy illustration looked like something right out of Middle Earth.

"Do you want to go to that?"

She looked up to find him watching her.

"I don't know. I haven't really thought about it," she said. She wasn't going to admit that the price was way out of her league.

"Since I'm performing, I get an extra ticket. You can have it if you want."

"Really?" She knew she was gushing, but who could be cool when someone was offering a *free* Pandemonium ticket? "You don't mind?"

"No, not at all."

She wanted to squeal like a four-year-old girl, but he hardly noticed. His attention was on the food. He lifted the panini-press top to reveal two perfectly browned, crisp sandwiches. He put them on plates and ladled soup from the pot on the stove into bowls. He set a bowl and plate in front of her. "I hope you like tomato and red pepper soup."

She already knew from the smell she was going to love it, but her mind was still reeling about the ball.

"So what's the deal with the costumes?" she asked and took a bit of the soup. "Is there a theme, or anything goes? Wow, where did you get this soup?"

She was going to track it down and buy a gallon.

"I made it a couple days ago. It's always better a day or two later. The flavors mingle. You shouldn't let your sandwich get cold."

She tried not to stare in disbelief, but really? He made it?

"Where'd you learn to cook like this?"

He sat down at a stool against the kitchen island and dipped the corner of his sandwich into the thick soup. "My aunt was a great cook. My dad, too. He used to tell me a man needed to know three things: how to make his own food, clean his own clothes, and balance his own budget. If he couldn't do those things, he'd always be at someone else's mercy."

"Sage advice," she said.

"Yeah," he said, and his expression turned solemn. He ran his hand over his head, pulling his dusky hair back from the hard planes of his face. The gaze of his forest-green eyes had drifted away, across years, she suspected, not miles.

He was so distant now, and she realized how much he must miss his parents.

"So, the ball," he said finally. "As far as costumes go, just about anything goes: a Halloween costume or a dance costume would work. The more outrageous the better, though."

"I can manage that." She mentally catalogued her dance wardrobe. "Anything else I need to know?"

He finished a bite from his sandwich. "Nothing comes to mind. How about you? Anything I should know?"

"I want my own bathroom," she said.

His eyebrows shot up, then he smiled. "All right. I can manage that."

Emboldened, she moved to the next item on her mental list. "I want a key."

He reached around, pulled something from his back pocket, and placed it on the counter beside her. It was a shiny, new brass key. "Already done. And the security code is the street number."

"Nice." She picked it up and turned it over in her hand. It was cold and solid and very, very real. How many women would envy this? But she couldn't think that way. This was business. That was it.

"Anything else?" he asked.

"Nope. My own room, my own bathroom, and a key. That's it."

Taz fidgeted. "Well, you'll have your own room until Gina gets here. Then you'll need to share my room."

She put down the spoonful of soup that was halfway to her mouth. "No way. This isn't going to be a friends-with-benefits kind of thing. If that's what you thought, that is not what this is."

He shook his head, amused. "Believe me, I'm not expecting that. But if my sister sees we're not sharing a room, she'll know we're not for real."

"How could she possibly know? It's not like she's going to inspect the house."

"You don't know my sister. That's the least she'll do. She's not coming here to visit Disneyland. She's coming to stick her nose in my business."

This guy really was paranoid. "Don't you think you're exaggerating?" He looked so glum, she punched his arm playfully. "She just wants to meet her little brother's special girl. That's all. And she'll only be popping in and out, right? It's not like she'll be staying here."

His gaze slipped away.

"She won't be staying here, right?"

"Actually, she is."

What an interesting piece of news he hadn't shared.

"You told me she was going to stay in a hotel."

His gaze dodged hers again. "I know. I tried, but she wouldn't go for it."

"So she'll be here. With us. Watching us every minute?"

He turned to the refrigerator and busied himself by pouring them each a glass of lemonade. "Not every minute. Just the couple of weeks she's here."

She couldn't have heard that right. "Wait, you just said you didn't know how long she was going to be here."

He was still turned away from her. "She said maybe two weeks, give or take."

CHAPTER ELEVEN

"TWO WEEKS? THAT'S how long we have to keep up this charade?" She started running through her calendar. She'd assumed three days, four tops. But two weeks? Maybe three? How in the world could they keep a lie going that long?

She was about to say so when he turned back. Her complaint died on her tongue. He wasn't smiling or sheepish. Now his eyes were narrowed, his shoulders squared, his jaw tense. "Yes," he said, any hint of remorse gone. "Two weeks, give or take. Is that going to be a problem?"

She leaned back and hit the edge of the counter with a thud. "I just wasn't expecting it to go that long."

"Well, there's still time to back out." He turned back to the fridge. She watched the wide span of his shoulders and the muscles tensing beneath his snug white T-shirt. Yeah, she should leave. This was obviously a mistake. Another to add to her ever-growing collection.

He turned back and seemed to sense her thoughts. The hard glare in his eyes had softened. "Before you go, I want you to see something first."

She put down her half-eaten sandwich and followed him to the staircase and up the curve of floating white steps to the second floor. He led her along a white corridor that glowed orange from the setting sun till he reached the last door. He opened it and stood aside for her to enter.

"This is my bedroom," he said.

She slanted a look at him, but it was clear he wasn't suggesting anything. Tentatively, she stepped into the vast cavern of a room, filled with the twilight glow glancing off the ocean. There was a king-sized bed wrapped in white linens and sky-blue pillows, a sleek dresser and matching nightstands in cool wood tones, and a giant potted palm tree in a corner. It was a gorgeous room but still paled in comparison to the view. Through the floor-to-ceiling windows, she could see the wide, blue sky meet the sparkling Pacific along the horizon. From this vantage point, it was like there was nothing between her and the ocean.

"This is beautiful," she said, aware that it was a ridiculous understatement, but unable to think of any other way to describe it. Breathtaking, maybe? Hypnotic?

She sensed him moving closer. The warmth of his body touched her, and she shivered.

"It's pretty nice," he said. "But this is what I wanted to show you." He stepped over to the navy-blue suede couch that sat in front of a sitting area arranged beside the room's white marble fireplace.

"A new sofa?" Seemed like a strange thing for a guy like Taz to be excited about. *Okay, so he's into interior design.* It wouldn't be the strangest thing she'd learned about him today.

"It's not just a sofa." He pulled the two seat cushions to the floor, reached down, and lifted out a foldaway bed.

Now she understood. "That's your solution?"

He was looking at her with such a soft, please-approve expression, it melted the snide comment tickling her tongue. He really was trying to make this work.

"Okay," she said, "but you're sleeping there, right? I get the bed."

The shadows lifted from his expression, and he smirked. "I was thinking we could alternate. Seems only fair."

She walked to the bed and fell back on it, throwing her arms wide. "No way, the bed is mine."

"Bed hog," he growled, but the humor was back in his voice. "Fine, but you better not be one of those grumpy morning people."

"Are you kidding? Of course I am. I'm awful until I've had at least two cups of coffee." She laughed, but it was sort of the truth. "What about you? You don't snore, do you?"

He faked a huge, honking snore. "Just like that. Every night. That won't bother you, will it?"

He walked by her, and she tried to kick his legs out from under him. He stumbled and dropped beside her. He shifted around.

"Hey, this bed really is comfortable. I take it all back. You're getting the hide-a-bed."

She rolled on top of him and pinned him. "Uh-uh, drummer boy. I already called dibs."

He brought his hands together, raised them between her arms, and knocked away her hands. She landed with a thump on his chest. Her laughter caught in her throat. She could feel his breath and smell the woodsy, pine scent of him. Her heart beat faster, but she knew it didn't have anything to do with their game anymore. She jumped up and was on the floor in an instant. She pretended to be immersed in the view. "Fine, we'll trade off. You're right, it's only fair." She swatted at invisible dust on her sleeves and invisible wrinkles in her black capri pants. Anything to keep from looking at those deep, green eyes of his.

He propped himself up. If he realized she was freaked out, he didn't say anything. "All right. Glad you can be reasonable. How about I show you the rest of the house?"

He slid off the bed and went to the door. She followed him down the hall.

The next door opened to another impossibly large room, and it was empty except for a stereo cabinet along one wall and a long, red-velvet tufted bench. She stepped in, and her heels made a clicking sound on the wooden floor. White plantation shutters covered the wide band of high windows. Two full walls were covered in mirrors. She pirouetted. "You have a dance room!" It was about half the size of the one at the studio, but more than enough for her. She turned and posed and played with her reflection.

"If I'd known you were such a narcissist, I would have showed you this room first."

"You should have," she gushed, gliding through the opening combinations of her audition choreography. "You probably would have gotten the bed without a fight."

"In that case, I re-pose the question—"

"Oh no," she said. "Too late for that. That issue is decided. We're taking turns. But this room, am I allowed to use it?"

"Yeah, if you want. Any time."

She bit back a goofy grin. It was almost too good to be true.

"I never use this room," he said. "The acoustics aren't great, so I created a sound-proof music room on the other side of the house."

She perked up. "You have a music room, too? Can I see it?"

She knew she was acting like a fangirl, but it was just so cool. She followed him down the hall. On the other side of the staircase, he opened a door to reveal a room that was half the size of the dance room but outfitted like a recording studio. Speakers, amplifiers, microphones, cables, and decks with dozens of knobs, levers, and gauges.

She recognized his signature *doumbek* against one wall, but there were others, too, as well as an acoustic guitar, a mandolin, and some horns. She reached up to touch the thick, charcoal-gray foam that covered the walls.

"That's what I call the 'neighbor savers,'" he said.

She looked at him funny, and he added, "Soundproofing. There's a window back there somewhere too, but the foam covers it. It keeps the sound levels down when I'm practicing, which keeps the neighbors happy."

She feigned surprise. "You mean they aren't music fans?"

"Not at two in the morning, which is usually the only time I have to work on anything here."

She approached the deck. "I didn't know you recorded your own work." Her fingers trailed over the levers and knobs.

"I don't really. I mean, I'm going to. Someday. I'm sort of working on something."

"Another Belly Dance Diva compilation? I'm not surprised. Dancers love it. You must be selling a ton."

He rubbed his chin. "It's not exactly for the Belly Dance Divas. It's something personal I'm working on. Some rhythms my father used to play with me when I was a kid, and some he used to do with his band. I'm adding them to some fusion beats, and I'm hoping to be able to release them as a solo album."

His smile was gone. He was tense again, back to being all business.

"Sounds cool. I'm sure it'll be just as popular as the Divas album. Anything you do with a drum is going to get attention. Wait, did that come out wrong?"

He chuckled. "I don't know, but I know what you mean."

"When are you going to release it?"

He ran his hand through his hair. "I was hoping to get it done this year, to coincide with the new Diva compilation—which is in the works, by the way—so it could dovetail with the marketing Garrett is planning for that release. But it doesn't look like that's going to happen. I need to get the master recordings back from my dad's old label, and so far I haven't been able to make that happen." That distant look came back, but just as quickly, he shrugged it off. "C'mon. We should probably get back to our food before it gets cold."

She grabbed some loose skin at her middle. "I don't think I'd suffer from a missed meal. I could probably use it."

"Watching your girlish figure?" he said as they made their way down the staircase.

She laughed. "Well, if I don't, no one else will either."

"Don't be so sure," he said. "Your curves are in all the right places."

"Oh, my," she said with exaggeration. "A compliment from Taz the Romancer himself. Imagine that."

He spun around with a sharp look. "Taz the what?"

She tapped him playfully on the arm again. "The Romancer. Don't tell me you've never heard that before."

He shook his head.

"You know, because you like the ladies?" She drawled out the last word and wiggled her fingers. He was obviously not seeing the humor in it, though. With more caution, she said, "No one says it in a bad way. It's just supposed to be funny. You know, a joke." She regretted saying anything, but it was too late to take it back. "I'm not saying you're a joke. I didn't mean—"

He turned away abruptly and took the remaining steps in twos. "Can we just drop it?"

The words felt like a slap in the face.

He ran his hand through his hair again and looked at his watch. "You know, I forgot I have an appointment. Help yourself to anything you find in the kitchen, unpack, do whatever." He turned back to her as she reached the last stair step. "I emptied half the dresser and half the closet. If you need more space, we'll work it out when I get back."

She watched his back because he was already halfway to the foyer. He grabbed a set of keys from a table and was standing in the open door. "Think you can handle it?"

She nodded. What else was she going to do? "I'll be fine." The words nearly choked her.

She heard the door shut and latch, and a moment later the roar of his Porsche. Then silence again. Just her, this massive house, and then a distinct and insistent sound of scratching coming from behind the kitchen door.

CHAPTER TWELVE

MELANIE FROZE WHERE she stood. What was that sound? She waited, every nerve, every muscle focused on the door. Now that she was alone, Taz's house didn't seem bright and open. It was stark. And white. And strange. Like a hospital. Or a laboratory.

There it was again. *Scratch-scratch. Scratch-scratch.*

Then a moan. Or was it a whimper?

She stared at the door and tried to breathe. Should she leave? Should she scream? The last thing she wanted to do was wind up on the eleven o'clock news—some horrible corpse found lying in a pool of blood on this ridiculously clean, white-tiled floor. She could already hear the neighbors being interviewed: "Never saw her before. Must have been a prowler. Must have been her own fault."

Scratch-scratch. Whimper.

Oh, for Pete's sake. She was not going out that way. She marched to the marble fireplace on the far side of the room and grabbed an iron poker as long as her leg. She sure as hell wasn't going out without a fight.

"Who's there?" she shouted at the closed door.

Silence.

"I'm warning you, I'm armed. You should just leave while you can."

Another scratch. Another moan.

It wasn't on the other side of this door. The sound was too distant. She pushed through the swinging door and heard it again. She stopped and listened. Another scratch. It was behind a door across the room. A closet?

Slowly, she stepped again. Closer.

Another scratch, then a jingle and a yip.

She dropped the baseball-batter stance and waited to be sure. She inched closer to the door and held her ear to it.

Another yip. More jingling. More scratching.

She smiled at her own stupidity and set the poker on the counter. She unlocked the door and cracked it open. Instantly, a tiny black nose pushed its way through.

She opened the door wider to find a small Yorkie with a black ribbon holding a spray of hair like a tiny fountain atop its head.

"Look at you," Melanie cooed as the toy-sized canine jumped to her knees. She bent and tried to pick him up, but the dog wanted nothing to do with her. He ran around Melanie's legs and across the kitchen floor to a corner, where there was a bowl of water and another with kibble. The dog slurped greedily at the water.

"Slow down there, little guy, you're going to drown yourself."

The mat beneath the bowls read "Spike."

"Spike, huh? Awfully menacing for a cutie-pie like you."

The dog lifted his head and stared.

"Sorry. You're right. I should learn to keep my big mouth shut. How about we start over? I'm Melanie, and it looks like I'm your new roommate."

CHAPTER THIRTEEN

THE SEAT BENEATH Taz rumbled. He tightened his grip on the Porsche's steering wheel and stared at the black-asphalt ribbon of Pacific Coast Highway passing beneath him.

"Left turn ahead," said a feminine, slightly British voice.

The car's navigation system—he'd dubbed her Sheila—was trying to steer him toward the Sultan's Tent. It was a route he'd set days ago, and he'd been letting it run, as he usually did, just to hear her voice. She didn't have everything KITT from *Knight Rider* had, but she was close enough for him. He'd saved every penny from that first year touring with the Divas to buy her. On his own, with no bank or loan from his sister. Sheila was his. So far, she'd proved herself to be the most dependable thing in his life.

Right now, however, even her reassuring voice wasn't making him feel better.

He tapped the cancel button on the navigation screen embedded in the dashboard. "Sorry, Sheila," he muttered and revved the engine.

He focused on the road, letting the restaurants, art galleries, and multimillion-dollar estates blur into the landscape.

Slowly, the things Melanie had said—the painful reminder that he hadn't always made the smartest choices—they burned away, too. Pushed farther into the crystal-clear horizon with every passing mile. Pushed until there was nothing but him, the car and the feeling of leaving it all behind.

The feeling carried him nearly to the San Diego County line, where the highway merged with the freeway. It was impossible to see the horizon now, swallowed by the blackness that hung over the Pacific. He knew he should go back and face her. He should have just been a man about it and said, "I've heard the name, so what?"

But he hadn't. He couldn't.

The truth was, he hated that name. Taz the Romancer, like he was some kind of gigolo, not just a guy who happened to date a lot. There was no crime in that. And what else was he supposed to do after Tamara left? Sit around and sulk? Hole up somewhere like a monk?

No way. At first he'd gone out so she'd know he wasn't pining. He'd never give her that satisfaction. But then it became easy, even natural. As simple as it had been to be with her, it became just as simple to be with lots of hers. There was also the side benefit of never having to worry that one day he might walk in on a business meeting that really had nothing to do with business at all. At least not his business.

He winced, remembering that day. Walking in on Tamara and that sleazy show promoter in their hotel room. That was the day he realized Tamara didn't love him—probably never had loved him. She loved the idea of being famous, and he was just a way to get there.

But Melanie didn't know any of that, and it had been stupid to leave tonight so suddenly. She hadn't meant to ridicule him. He knew that. Why did it matter what she thought anyway? They weren't dating. They weren't even friends, not really.

But for some reason it still bothered him.

He pulled off the highway, onto a small dirt road overlooking the shore. He couldn't see much of the surf, but he could hear the rhythm of the waves. The roaring and the crashing, over and over again. The repetition soothed him in the way the ocean always soothed him. It made him feel like any problem he had was nothing more than one grain of sand among the billions and trillions along the shore.

He should go back home. Maybe he should apologize. Maybe he should ask if they could start again.

Maybe, but not now.

He parked in a deserted lot overlooking the beach and sat, looking out over the steering wheel. He lowered the window to let the cool breeze blow in from the surf. It whipped his hair about his face, and he breathed in the cold, salty air as he listened to the surf. The roar and the crash... the roar and the crash... the roar and the crash.

That was the thing he loved best about the ocean. It made him think there was time for anything. There was all the time in the world.

CHAPTER FOURTEEN

WHEN MELANIE'S ALARM on her smartphone went off at seven in the morning, she'd meant to tap the snooze button. It came as a startling surprise to discover those luxurious eight extra minutes of sleep had somehow become two hours. She leaped from the guest-room bed and scrambled to find her suitcase and something to wear to work.

Spike didn't move from her cozy spot in the bed. She watched Melanie hop around the floor, trying to tug a pencil skirt up over her hips.

"What are you lookin' at?" Melanie grumbled. "It's his fault, you know."

She was already in bed and asleep when the sound of distant drumming had awoken her around midnight. It had taken a few disoriented moments to remember where she was and that the drumming was coming from the music room down the hall. Her first instinct was to get up and apologize for her earlier, careless insult. But what should she say?

She mentally played through a few apologies and rejected each one. Wouldn't it just make things worse to bring it up again? Instead, she'd lain there, listening to him play. It was easy to do because the music was good. Actually, it was great, like nothing she'd ever heard before.

She'd been happy to stay awake and listen—at least she had been until the alarm went off at seven. Then she didn't want anything more than to remain under the incredibly comfortable, incredibly warm covers.

Hitting the wrong button just made her morning a whole lot worse.

Once the skirt was up and a shirt was on, she yanked a brush through her hair and pulled it back in a ponytail. The easiest and quickest remedy for a terrible case of bed head.

When she emerged from the guest room with her purse slung over her shoulder, she paused in front of the door to the music room, stunned by the sight of him in the chair in front of the mixing board and computer screen.

"When you pull an all-nighter, you really pull—"

A soft, gentle snore interrupted her.

"Taz?" she said as she inched into the room. His elbows were on the table, and his chin was cradled in his hands. His chest rose and fell with each breath, but otherwise he was completely still. "You awake?"

She took another step. He snored softly again.

She bent her head to see his face, his eyes closed, his dark lashes resting against the rise of his cheeks. He looked... peaceful.

She smiled to herself and backed out of the room.

The first thing she saw when she stepped off the elevator at the office was her boss going through her inbox.

"Good morning," she said warily. It wasn't often that she found him thumbing through her things. "Are you looking for something?"

"Well, of course I'm looking for something," Carl Deffner blasted back. His face was flushed around his temples, and his nostrils flared.

"Okay," she said more cautiously as she set her purse down on the desk corner. "If you tell me what it is, maybe I can help."

He'd already tugged a stapled stack of white papers out of the pile. "This is it. The budget forecast. I forgot we have a department review today. I need the report by one."

She stared at the stack. "That'll take hours. It'll take all day, at least a day."

He shrugged and walked back to his office. "I have to have it for the meeting. I know you'll make it work. You always do."

You always do. Yeah, because she worked her butt off. She came in early, worked through lunch, and stayed late. All so Deffner could look good to his boss. Sure, he'd saved her a few times from the layoff list, but lately she was beginning to wonder if it was even worth it.

Four hours later, her eyeballs felt like they were covered in starch from staring at the computer so long, but at least Deffner was happy. He'd been so relieved when she handed him the finished report, he hadn't even balked when she said she was going to take the afternoon off.

"Not feeling well, Drake?" he asked, pulling on his worn brown blazer, his typical attire for an executive-floor meeting.

When she didn't answer right away, he added, "It's not one of those female complaints, is it? Wait, don't tell me. I don't want to know."

That wasn't exactly the excuse she'd come up with, but it would do. She sucked in her lips and stayed silent.

"Just forward my phone to voice mail before you leave." And he was gone.

When she'd packed up, she checked her to-do list to be sure she hadn't forgotten anything. Everything was checked off. Everything but one thing: the audition registration. The thing she thought about every day but still hadn't done.

She couldn't tell herself there wasn't time. She had all afternoon.

She couldn't tell herself she'd do it later. How much later could she wait?

If she was going to do it, it had to be now.

It was going to be now.

CHAPTER FIFTEEN

WHATEVER COMPLAINT TAZ had about the dance room's acoustics was not evident to Melanie as she twisted and twirled through her choreography. It was a glorious dance space, a perfect dance space. She could hardly believe it was all hers, at least for a while.

She was still trying to wrap her mind around it. It felt like a dream, like at any time, she could wake up and discover she was back in that room in her mom's trailer, listening to the whir of cars zipping over the freeway overpass.

It was heaven, dancing here with the lights low and the music loud, with no one watching but Spike in the corner, who it turned out was a girl after all.

The music nudged Melanie, pushing her one way then another. She liked to imagine the rhythm as a flesh-and-blood partner. She played with it, and teased it. She felt it engulf her, moving her hips, her feet, her arms, her chest. At the end of the slow melody, the *taksim*, she struck a pose, bent into a bow, and felt the last ounce of energy drain away from her.

The music continued to fade, slowly, slowly, until it melted completely into silence.

The sound of clapping broke the spell. She snapped her head up, and Taz was there, casually leaning against the open doorway, as though he had been there awhile. Spike noticed him, too. The dog yipped, jumped, and ran to his owner's black leather boots.

"You've met Spike?" Taz said, smiling. He bent down to scratch behind the dog's perked-up ears. "I didn't know if you were a dog person, so I left her in the garage until we sorted things out. Right, Spikey? Right?"

Something dopey and adorable happened to people when they were around small, cute animals. Apparently it happened to world-famous drummers, too.

"I think Spike had other ideas," Melanie said. She stared at the red polish on her toenails. "I want to apologize for what I said yesterday. Sometimes my brain takes a vacation while my mouth is still moving. I didn't mean—"

His hand shot up, and he shook his head. "Don't worry about it. I know people talk."

He looked like he wanted to say more, but he didn't.

She changed the subject before she could say anything else she'd regret. "How long have you had Spike? She's so cute."

"A couple years," he said, scratching the dog's belly. Spike had rolled onto her back and nipped at the air in what looked like complete and utter euphoria. "She used to be Gina's. She left her behind when she moved to New York. Her building doesn't allow pets."

"She must miss her. I mean, look at her. She's the definition of cute."

The little thing was wiggling and preening now, like she knew she was being praised.

"She's pretty smart, too. Watch." Taz flipped his finger in a circle, and the dog rolled over. He clapped and the dog sat up, straight as a razor. Taz made a gun with his thumb and forefinger. "Bang!" he said, and Spike rolled onto her side and played dead.

When Taz said, "Okay," Spike bounced up and wiggled again.

"Good girl," Taz said and rubbed her ears.

"Guess you aren't the only one with talent in this house," Melanie said. "So I've been getting acquainted with the house, and I have to ask, what's with all the white? This place is like a museum. I'm afraid to touch anything."

He chuckled. "You'll get over it. Right now you see white, but after a while, you'll notice the colors. In the morning, it's yellow. Around noon, it's more blue. At sunset, you get the warm orange, then violet. Eventually, we get all the colors of the spectrum in here. That was my dad's plan, anyway."

"I didn't think of it that way," she said, chastened. There she went, sticking her foot in her mouth again. "I guess I'm just not used to it. I'm used to tiny, dingy apartments. Tiny, dingy trailers. Tiny windows, if I'm lucky. All this wide-open, airy space, I'm just not used to it."

She thought she saw him shudder. Compact spaces had never bothered her. She kind of preferred them. She had lived in larger places—nothing as large as his house—but the house where they had lived before Dad left was a two-story, four-bedroom house with a pool in the backyard. It was what some people probably considered a suburban dream home. What she remembered most about living there, though, was the hours spent cleaning it. Every Saturday morning she had her list of chores: vacuum, dust, clean the windows and mirrors, and sweep. Between her and her mother, they cleaned that house every weekend, from the floorboards to the ceiling corners, until it practically sparkled. Her mother would beam when it was finished, but all Melanie could think about was the fun her friends were having without her. She would rather have gone to the mall, to the park, or anywhere really. But no, she was stuck in that house with a sponge or a mop in her hand.

There was one silver lining when Dad had left and Mom moved them into the trailer: there was less to clean. But even that silver lining lost its appeal pretty quickly when her mom's cleaning routine dropped from obsessive to nil.

Still, Melanie appreciated the low maintenance and minimal effort that went into small spaces. Or maybe she'd just gotten used to them. Maybe that's why she gravitated to the dance room. It wasn't as grand as the rest of the house. It was simple, and it was cozy.

"I hope you don't mind that I'm in here," she said.

He shook his head. "Not at all. No one has used it since my mom passed away."

"Is that her?" Melanie pointed to a trio of black-and-white photos of a belly dancer, the only artwork in the room.

"That's my grandmother," he said. "Those pictures were taken in Cairo in 1946 or '47. That's Badia Masabni's nightclub. It's where my grandfather met my grandmother."

Melanie gazed at the image with renewed interest. "Your grandmother danced in Badia Masabni's company? Did she know Samia Gamal?"

He pulled back in surprise. "You know who Samia Gamal is?"

"Of course," she said. "She's practically my hero. I used to copy her choreography and her costumes when I first started performing. I had an exact replica made of the costume she wore in *Afrita Hanem*. All flowing chiffon and sequins."

"What changed?"

"People kept thinking I was impersonating *I Dream of Jeannie*, so I stopped and moved on."

He shook his head. "Not many people know about the old days. Not even many dancers."

"Their loss," she said. "New isn't always better. Hey, who's this?" She pointed to another photograph. It had worn into rust tones, like it was from the 1970s or earlier.

"That's my mom. It was taken in New York, when she used to dance with my father's orchestra. It was '65, I think."

"She's gorgeous, too." She recognized the high cheekbones. Taz had inherited them, and her wide, expressive eyes.

"Yeah, and she was a pretty terrific dancer. She trained a lot of the dancers who became famous in the 1970s, but she gave up dancing almost entirely when she had my sister and I. She was just starting to teach again when…"

He didn't need to finish the sentence. Melanie knew. The airliner crash that had taken his parents' lives was well known in belly dance circles. It had catapulted their already considerable fame into legend.

"I'm sorry," she whispered.

He smiled, but she could see the pain in his eyes. "She never said she regretted giving up her career, but I know she made time to dance every day of her life. When she was here or when she was in New York. Even if she was in a hotel, she would sneak downstairs and find an empty ballroom or open conference room, and she would dance to nothing but the memory of music. I think dancing was as important to her as breathing. It was who she was."

"She must have been a very special lady," she said, touching his arm, trying to draw him back from the past. "If I had a room like this, I wouldn't stop dancing either." She stepped into the center of the room and twirled, as if that proved her point.

A hint of a smile tugged at the corners of his mouth. "It's nice to see someone using the space again. It's been a long time."

"I can honestly say it is my pleasure." She twirled again.

"You're really good, you know."

She stopped twirling. "Really?" she asked hopefully. She blushed, embarrassed. With thick sarcasm, she added, "You aren't getting all sweet on me now, are you?"

She wanted to sink into a black hole and never come out. Why had she said that?

But now he was blushing.

"I mean your dancing," he said. "You have a lot of promise."

Of course he hadn't meant *her*. He dated Divas. He wouldn't be interested in her. She played it cool. "I do declare," she said in a false Southern accent, "has Mr. Taz Roman complimented little ol' me?"

He grinned. Whatever dark shadows had gathered in his expression were gone now. "I didn't say there wasn't work to do."

She straightened. "Work? Like what kind of work?"

"Don't get defensive," he cajoled. "That's why you're here, right? To learn?"

"Yeah, but…" What was the point of arguing? Of course that's why she was here. It was the only reason she was here. She couldn't forget that.

"Fine. So if you're gonna help, then what do you suggest?"

Damn. He looked so cocky now, leaning against the doorjamb with that high-and-mighty smirk.

She looked away.

"Well," he said coolly, "the first piece of advice I'd give you is that you rush your moves. They're good, don't get me wrong, but they're too fast."

"That's not true," she snapped back. "I'm always on the beat."

He cocked his head to the side. "You're getting defensive."

"I'm not. You're just wrong."

His eyes widened. "So this is you not being defensive? Fine, forget I said anything." He raised his hands and backed into the hall.

That was it? He was giving up?

"Wait," she said to the empty space in the doorway. "I'm sorry. Finish what you were saying."

He leaned back into view. "Are you sure?"

"Yes. I'm sure. I need to slow down. What else?"

"Not exactly slow down, but don't anticipate the music so much. It's only when you're dancing to recorded music. You were perfect when you danced with me at the Tent."

"I was?" That was news to her. He hadn't said anything about that performance. "You think I was perfect?"

"When you use recorded music," he said, "you probably know it so well that you're focusing on what's coming, not what's there. What you want to do is let the music pull you along, not the other way around. If the audience notices you anticipating the changes, they register it. Even if it's a split second, they sense that you're out of sync. It disrupts the flow."

She stared at him blankly. It wasn't as though she'd expected him to shout, "You're the best dancer ever! Garrett will beg you to be in the Divas!" But it didn't dampen the sting of the criticism. "Okay, I got it. Anything else?"

He scratched the evening stubble on his chin.

There was more. Great. The way his eyes roamed over her. She knew that look. It was the same one she got from strangers on the street. The one she got from her own mother after her first date with an ink gun. "It's the tattoos, isn't it?"

She'd been expecting this one. A few of the Divas had tattoos. Mostly belly art like swirls and vines that blended in with the costume. But no one had art on their arms and legs, like she did. Garrett might be open minded, but maybe he wasn't *that* open minded. "You're thinking I should cover them up, right?"

Taz's expression twisted. "No, that's not what I meant at all. It's the way you dance. There's too much ballet and not enough belly in your belly dance."

She certainly wasn't expecting that. She sneered. "There's no ballet in my dance."

He stepped backward again. "You're right. It's fine. Forget I said anything." He turned and shoved his hands in his front pockets.

"Don't leave. I didn't mean that. I mean, maybe you could tell me what you mean by 'too much ballet'?"

He turned back and hiked an eyebrow. "Your arms. They float too high. Bring them down a bit. Garrett prefers the dancers who focus on the hips, the belly, the center. He wants to see the shimmy, the drops, and the *uh-uh-uh.*" He accentuated the sound with three sharp shakes of his lean, denim-covered hips.

Now, there are male belly dancers. There are even some good male belly dancers, but Taz Roman was not one of them. She bit her lip, trying not to laugh.

He feigned a hurt look. "Hey, what's wrong with my *uh-uh-uh?*"

He did it again, and she had to turn away so she wouldn't erupt with laughter. When she'd recovered enough to speak, she said, "All right. I need to slow down and put more *uh-uh-uh* into the dance. I'll make a note."

The sound of the front door opening downstairs stopped her. A woman called out, "Hello, anyone home? Taz, are you home?"

His eyes widened in surprise, or was it fear?

"Who is it?" Melanie asked in a whisper.

The color disappeared from his face. "My sister."

CHAPTER SIXTEEN

"HURRY!" TAZ SAID, snapping into action. "Get your stuff out of the guest room and into my room. Throw your things in drawers or hang it up, I don't care. Just make it look like you live here."

Melanie froze.

"I'll go down and stall her," he said. "Come down as soon as you can. Go! Now!"

The panic in his eyes shocked her out of her paralysis. She didn't say anything but did as he said. She went to the guest room, grabbed her suitcase from beside the bed, and rolled it to his room. Downstairs, she heard him greet his sister.

"Look at you!" came the woman's high-pitched reply. "Are you surprised? I knew you would be."

His answer was lost in a mumble.

"Where is she?"

Melanie strained to listen as she worked.

"I have to meet this mystery woman of yours."

Oh no! The voices grew closer. Were they on the stairs? In the hall? Melanie stared at the pile of clothes she had dumped out of her suitcase onto the bed.

"Have you done anything with Daddy's den? Oh! A music room. Very nice. What about Mommy's dance room? Of course not. Where are you hiding her, this new lady of yours?"

"Her name is Melanie. I told you that, and I'm pretty sure she's sleeping. We shouldn't disturb her."

"Don't be such a worrywart. She won't mind. We're practically family, right?"

The bedroom door swung open to reveal a slender woman with smooth, porcelain skin and cascading chocolate-brown hair. She wore an ivory silk blouse with a wide, leather belt that accentuated her narrow waist and hips. The hem of a pair of cleanly tailored pants brushed the tops of her wedge sandals, and a bib of gold chains wrapped her collar. Every inch of her screamed sophistication. Very East Coast. Very New York.

As surprised as Melanie was to see her intruders, it was nothing compared to the surprise on Gina's face when Melanie lifted herself from the bed covers and pretended to yawn.

"Oh, hello." She squinted and rubbed imaginary sleep from her eyes. She tugged up the collar of the white velour robe she'd found hanging on the back of the bedroom door. "Taz, honey, I'm sorry. Did I oversleep?"

Taz pushed into the room. "Melanie, uh, this is Gina, my sister. She wanted to surprise us."

"Surprise!" Gina declared with a broad smile and threw her arms out wide.

"She, uh, wanted to say hello," Taz said.

"I would have been here hours ago, but my connecting flight was delayed in Denver."

Melanie shot Taz a wide-eyed look. At least they'd dodged *that* disaster.

If Gina noticed, it didn't show. "If it had been Chicago," she added, "it would have been fine. But Denver? What can anyone do for five hours in Denver? Then it was impossible to find a decent car service. I had to rent something, and you know how much I hate to drive in LA.

"We'll let you get back to your nap. Right, Gina?" He put his hands on his sister's shoulders and steered her back to the door.

"Right," Gina said reluctantly. "I guess we'll see you downstairs."

She let Taz push her back toward the hall, and Melanie faked another yawn. She caught Taz's eye on the way out and winked. He smiled.

A few moments later, she heard a soft knock on the door before it opened. She dropped the suitcase she had stuffed down beside the bed, out of view.

"Oh, it's you. Is the coast clear?"

Taz shut the door and shook his head in disbelief. "That was incredible."

She posed and bowed. "Did you enjoy this evening's performance?"

"I have never seen Gina speechless before. It was great. It was better than great. She's really going to hate you."

The comment should have made her happy. That was the point, right? "Happy to oblige," she said. "It's why I'm here. Where is she now?"

He jutted his chin toward the door. "Down in the kitchen, getting reacquainted with Spike. I think she's pissed the dog doesn't seem to remember her. It's kind of hilarious."

"You're harsh," Melanie said.

He rolled his eyes. "Believe me, it's nothing close to what she dishes out. You'll see."

"Anyway, she won't come back up any time soon, so I think you're safe for now. Come down when you're ready. Actually, she's probably hungry from her flight and will want something to eat."

Melanie was still comfortably full from their early dinner. "What about your soup? I'll bet they didn't serve anything that good on her flight."

"She doesn't eat leftovers, and I'm really not in the mood to put something together. I'll just take her out."

"Or I could make something," Melanie offered. Wait, what? She didn't cook. Unless you counted mac and cheese out of a box.

He shook his head. "It's nice of you to offer, but we're trying to make a bad impression, remember?"

"Right. Bad impression. So what should I wear?"

"Whatever you want or nothing at all. That'd suit me just fine." He smirked.

She pulled a wad of clothing from the pile she had stuffed beneath the sheets and hurled it at him.

He grabbed it in mid-air and let the two tank tops and pair of yoga pants fall to the ground. Still in his hand was her laciest black bra. He lifted it and gave it an approving look. "Yeah, now this is what I'm talking about." He tossed it back on the bed. "Definitely wear that."

"Go!" She pointed to the door and gave him her sternest, most reprimanding look.

He laughed. "See you downstairs, sweetheart," he said, sarcasm dripping from the word, and he shut the door behind him.

She dropped back against the pillows and stared at the white, coffered ceiling. What in the world had she gotten herself into?

CHAPTER SEVENTEEN

"WE'LL FOLLOW YOU to the restaurant," Taz told Gina as he left the house with Melanie in tow.

Gina shook her head. "I rented an Escalade. There's plenty of room for all of us."

Taz stared at the white behemoth parked in the driveway. He shook his head. It was just like her to show up in a monstrosity like that.

"Couldn't you get anything bigger?"

"Keep your sarcasm to yourself," Gina shot back. "You know I hate that tiny toy car you drive."

"A Porsche Carrera is hardly a toy."

Gina twirled her finger in the air. "Fine. It's a flashy car. I get it. Does that mean Garrett is paying you what you're worth, or are you just driving around in what was left of Mommy and Daddy's money?"

It didn't take long for her to revisit that old sore spot.

"I paid for that car myself, and you know it." It might be the only thing of value he'd been able to buy on his own, but damn it, he'd done it. The car was his and his alone. Still, the insinuation burned within him.

He looked back at Melanie, whose gaze was trained on the gray cobblestones in front of her. She was probably thanking heaven she was an only child all over again. He held back till she caught up to him. "You okay?"

Her head shot up. "Yeah, of course," she said then lowered her voice to a whisper. "Is she always like this?"

"Pretty much," he whispered back.

At the vehicle, he opened the passenger door and held it for Melanie to get in. When he turned to let himself into the driver's seat, Gina was already there.

"You don't think I'm handing the keys over to you, do you?"

"Wouldn't dream of it," he growled and made his way around to the front passenger seat. "Let's just have a nice dinner, all right?"

Gina smoothed her curls back over her shoulder when she settled in behind the wheel. "Of course we're going to have a nice dinner. Why wouldn't we have a nice dinner?" She looked for Melanie in the rear-view mirror. "I forgot how touchy he can be, but I'm sure I'm not telling you anything new. You live with it every day."

Great. Now she was recruiting Melanie to join her offensive. Just what he needed: two women on his case.

"Not really," Melanie said. "Taz is one of the most easygoing guys I know."

He glanced up and caught Melanie's eye. She smiled a quick flash of a smile, like a secret just between them.

He smiled back. She certainly didn't seem rattled by Gina. Maybe his sister had finally met her match.

He settled into his seat. If she could keep this up, this whole thing might just work. Who knows? The way she had looked all rumpled in his bed, covered in his blankets… it had been all he could do to keep his mind on the situation and off the image of her in that black, lacy bra. No. He couldn't think about that. He had to keep his cool and keep his head, or Gina would be on to him. She'd never give him any peace.

"You aren't angry that I got here a few days early, are you?" Gina said, guiding the Escalade out of the driveway. "But when I realized the Pandemonium Ball was this weekend, I had to come. Actually, I should be angry at you for not reminding me. You know how much I love that event. All the glitz and glamour. All those delicious costumes."

"That's why you're here?" he said. "I'm sure it's sold out by now. You should have checked before you flew out."

The lecture didn't faze Gina. "It's sold out for people who don't have connections. I have connections."

He shifted to look at her squarely. "You have connections?"

She shrugged. "Of course I do. Well, *a* connection. My brother is the star drummer with the Belly Dance Divas, and I hear he's performing. I'm sure he can get me in."

He dropped back in the seat. "So that's your answer? That I'll get you in? Sorry, Gina. It's not gonna happen. I get one comp ticket, and I've already given it to Melanie."

"Oh, c'mon, Taz," Gina said, picking up speed when they reached Coast Highway. "I know you've got some kind of bromance going with Garrett. I'm sure you can get him to give you one more ticket."

He rubbed his eyes. She hadn't even been here an hour, and they were right back to their old patterns. Her bossing him around, and him taking it. Unless he put a stop to it. "No, Gina," he said, his fingertips gripping into the leather armrest. "I'm not begging for another pass for you. If you want to go so badly, you'll have to find your own way."

"I see," Gina said in the flat, cool tone that meant she was not giving up. Not yet. But she didn't say anything until she pulled up to the valet stand in front of the restaurant, and then it was only to the young man who took her keys.

CHAPTER EIGHTEEN

MELANIE WALKED WITH Taz as his sister led the way to La Vista's entrance. But if Melanie thought the drama was over for the evening, she was sorely mistaken.

The first place the hostess put them was at a table along the kitchen wall. If you didn't mind looking past a few more tables, it had a nice view of the Pacific and the restaurant's neatly tended rose garden.

That wasn't good enough for Gina Roman. The woman pointed to an empty one beside a window.

"I prefer that one," she said.

The hostess—impossibly tall, impossibly thin, and impossibly tan—smiled sweetly. "That one is reserved."

"This one is fine," Taz whispered through clenched teeth. He had already shaken off his jacket and was placing it across the back of his chair.

"No," Gina shot back. "It's not fine. Why should we have to sit hidden in the corner when there is a perfectly good table right there that isn't being used?"

The hostess's perma-smile vanished.

Melanie looked at Taz.

Taz turned to Gina. "She told you why," he grumbled. "It's *reserved*."

"I just don't understand. We're here now. We might even be finished by the time that party arrives." She turned a saccharine smile to the hostess. "I know. Why don't you fetch the manager? I'm sure he can sort this out."

The hostess seemed only too eager to oblige. She nodded and walked away so quickly Melanie thought she might break into a run. Not that she blamed her. She'd run too, if she could.

"Why do you always have to make a scene?" Taz complained. "Can't we just have a decent meal without all your drama for once?"

"What drama, Tazarian?" his sister replied coolly. "I'm simply not going to be a doormat. But, of course, I wouldn't expect you to understand."

"Hey, did you see that?" Melanie pointed out the window to the surf. "I think I just saw a dolphin playing in the waves." Honestly, it was too dark for her to see anything of the kind, but somebody had to steer this train away from the brick wall. It was the only thing that came to mind.

"How quaint," Gina said. "Just like a tourist. How long have you even lived in Orange County?" Gina spoke slowly, as though to a child.

"All my life," Melanie shot back.

Whether that did anything to improve Gina's opinion of her was hard to tell. It didn't matter, because a man in an impeccable navy suit was approaching them.

"Hello, good evening. Maria tells me you have requested a table that is unfortunately unavailable. However, we can have another, one closer to the window, ready in just a few moments. If you'd care to have a seat at the bar, I'd be delighted to offer you beverages while you wait. On the house, of course."

Gina turned up a wide, charming smile. "Now that is what I call service. See, Tazarian? All you have to do is ask."

A moment later, they were perched on stools outside, overlooking a gazebo and the long, grassy park that skirted the beachside cliffs, sipping margaritas in the candlelight and enjoying the warm night air.

Melanie tipped back the last of her double margarita. She thought it would be enough to fill the strained silence of her dinner party, but it wasn't quite doing the trick.

She was almost relieved when Gina, empty glass dangling between her fingers, said in a sing-song voice, "So, about the Pandemonium. Are you absolutely sure there's no way Garrett will shake loose another ticket? Just one?"

"No," Taz said flatly. "One comp ticket per performer, that's the rule. Always has been."

Gina rolled her eyes. "Sure, I can see that for the regular performers, but you're Taz Roman. He owes you a lot more than one complimentary ticket. Really, it's the least he can do."

"We're not having this discussion," he said. "Not now, and certainly not here."

Melanie wasn't sure if "here" meant the restaurant or in front of her. Either way, she wished she could shrink into a ball and roll somewhere beneath the white tablecloth.

Gina released an exaggerated sigh and pouted. "But Taz, you know how much it means to me. I came out early especially for the ball. Isn't there any way?" She perked up. "Wait. I know." She turned to Melanie. "You probably don't even want to go, right?"

"Gina!"

The smile dropped from Gina's expression. "What? Why should your one and only ticket go to someone who doesn't even want it?"

"I do want it," Melanie said.

"See?" he said to Gina.

The woman's gaze burned into Melanie.

Maybe Taz noticed, because he added, "If you'll drop it, I'll talk to Garrett. We've got a meeting tomorrow anyway. I just don't want to hear anything else about that stupid party tonight."

"Thank you, Tazarian," Gina chirped. "I knew I could count on you."

He disappeared with a grumble behind his menu.

Melanie fidgeted with the corner of hers. Gina was watching her like a hungry cat.

"So," Melanie said, trying not to feel like a helpless mouse, "Taz says you've been living in Manhattan for a few years now. How do you like it?"

"My husband's position requires us to live there. I do what I can to make it tolerable."

Taz muttered something beneath his breath. Gina ignored it, so Melanie did, too.

"You must miss the Southern California weather. It's hard to beat this, right?" She motioned to the window and the moonlight twinkling on the water.

Gina dabbed her straw into the new, slushy margarita a server set in front of her. "The scenery? Not very creative when it comes to conversation, are you? I suppose I shouldn't be surprised. Taz never did go for brainy types."

"Excuse me?" Melanie said, sure the woman could not have meant that to be as rude as it sounded.

The sharp words seemed to have no effect on Gina. "I have to say," she said, "I was rather expecting someone…" She leaned to the side to take in the rose and hibiscus tattoo that covered much of Melanie's left arm and the spray of cherry blossoms that climbed her calf. "A little different."

Melanie stiffened and kept the words she was thinking on lockdown. This woman was supposed to dislike her. Irritating as it was, this was working out exactly as it should. She breathed deeply and recalibrated the rage simmering inside her.

"I see you're admiring my tattoos." She straightened her leg and tugged up her black skirt to reveal more of the cherry blossoms climbing her thigh. "Do you have any? I love them. My ex-boyfriend is a tattoo artist. He gave me this one. He also did the cherry blossoms on my leg. I can't show you the whole thing, though." She looked around like a conspirator and lowered her voice. "We have to keep this family-friendly, right?" She laughed like she thought she was the funniest person alive.

Gina wasn't laughing. She actually sputtered a bit of her margarita. "I don't have any tattoos. Do I look like the…"

Taz coughed into his hand and leveled a stare at Gina that stopped her cold. She started again. "No, to answer your question, I have no tattoos." She glared at Taz. "Do you?"

He shook his head but grinned. "Not yet, but I'm thinking about it. I just can't decide what to get."

Melanie smiled then caught herself. She had to stop acting like a goofy schoolgirl. And she sure as hell shouldn't be feeling all tingly inside when he looked at her.

Luckily, Taz didn't seem to pick up on any of it. Before Gina could question him further, a waiter approached. "Your table is ready. If you'll follow me."

On the way, Melanie spied the hostess at her station, shaking her head and looking anywhere but Gina's direction.

Don't blame you, sister. I'd steer clear of us, too.

By the time they reached the table, Gina had finished her margarita and handed it to the waiter. "I'll take another, thank you."

Gina spent most of the meal complaining about the flight, the hassle of searching for a driving service, and then having to resort to a vehicle rental. Melanie half-listened and focused mostly on enjoying her halibut.

When they were taking their last bites, Gina pounced again.

"So how long have you lived in my house?" Gina said between nibbles of her papaya and avocado salad.

Uh-oh. Melanie turned to Taz. "Gosh, it seems like no time at all. How long has it been, sweetheart?"

She nearly stumbled on the word. He didn't flinch.

"Three months?" he said between bites of his wild-duck quesadilla. "No, wait. It has to be longer than that. Remember, it was just after the holidays."

Gina raised her eyebrows. "That long? In all that time, you never thought to share the news?"

He shrugged. "You're so busy with your dinner parties and weekends in Connecticut. I didn't think you'd be interested."

"Not interested in my baby brother's life? What kind of shrew do you think I am?"

Melanie was silently forming her own, curt answer to that question when Gina continued.

"But what am I doing?" Gina added. "We shouldn't be arguing. We should be celebrating." She lifted her margarita glass and waited patiently for them to clink their glasses with hers. "To the two of you," she said. "You are very lucky, Tazarian, to have found someone again."

Melanie perked. "Again?" She knew she shouldn't have said it, she shouldn't have said anything, but she couldn't help it. When did Taz the Romancer ever have a "someone"?

Taz's jaw tensed, and he stared out the window.

"It's been a while," Gina said, jumping in. "Tamara was a dancer, just like you." Her face twisted. "Well, not quite like you, but that's how they met, isn't it, Tazarian? It was love at first sight, if I remember correctly. At least it was for Taz. He was so smitten. Absolutely lovesick."

"Gina, that's enough." His words were low and menacing.

His sister batted them away like fuzzy cat toys.

"He's just being sensitive. I'm sure he's told you about her. They were inseparable for months. I thought for sure they were on their way to the altar. Actually, you did propose, didn't you?"

The thump on the table made everyone jump, including a few diners sitting around them. Gina's laughter died.

"I said that's enough," he muttered, surprisingly calm in the face of that violence.

Luckily for Gina, maybe luckily for all of them, the waiter arrived to check on the meal.

They all smiled and uttered some version of "fine, thank you." When the waiter left, the topic died beneath a request for salt and refills on the water.

After dinner, they drove back to the house in silence.

"Those margaritas really did me in," Gina said with an exaggerated yawn. "I think I'm going to turn in early and leave you two lovebirds alone."

Melanie searched Taz's expression for some clue as to what she was supposed to do. He offered nothing. She turned to Gina. "Is there anything I can get for you? Some water, fresh towels?" She realized she was offering things she had no clue how to provide. It just seemed like the sort of thing she should do.

"No, I can find what I need," Gina said. "Don't trouble yourself."

It was the kindest the woman had been to her all night.

When the woman disappeared up the stairs, Melanie turned to Taz. He hadn't spoken since dinner. Whatever nerve Gina had tweaked within him was still tweaked. Melanie sidled up to him with a smile and whispered, "How'd I do?"

He sighed. "About as well as could be expected, I guess. I'm going out." He walked back to the front door.

"Hey, wait," she cried. "What am I supposed to do?"

He opened the door and shook his head. "Whatever you want, I guess." The door shut behind him.

CHAPTER NINETEEN

MELANIE WAS TUCKED beneath the silky, white bed covers and surrounded by piles of soft pillows, watching a Samia Gamal movie she'd brought, when she heard the Porsche pull up to the front.

She muted the television and listened to the front door open, then close. Somewhere out there, Gina was roaming free. Melanie had run into her in the kitchen soon after Taz left. When the conversation immediately turned to how Melanie had met Taz, she feigned a headache and said she needed to lie down upstairs.

She knew it probably bordered on rude, but under the circumstances, it wasn't going to matter anyway.

And the thought of having that luxurious bathroom all to herself was too much to resist. She had taken a long shower and washed her hair. She used Taz's salon-label shampoo and conditioner instead of her own bargain brand. She donned a comfortable tank top and yoga pants and crawled into bed to watch the giant television screen hanging above his dresser.

If she could have picked up the phone and ordered room service, it would have been the nicest hotel she'd ever stayed in. Hell, even without room service, it was the nicest anywhere she had ever stayed.

She considered going down and making herself a hot cup of tea when her stomach growled an hour later, but the fear of running into Gina kept her in the room.

With the gray images moving on the screen like shadows, she listened for the sound of conversation below. Nothing. Just footsteps. Coming closer. The doorknob turned, and then the dark silhouette of Taz was in the doorway.

"Hope you don't mind me watching television in here," she said cautiously, watching for clues in his expression, his voice. He'd been angry when he left—was he still? Was he regretting what they'd done? She needed something to figure out where she stood in all this.

"There's a better TV downstairs," he said as he went to the closet. "Why are you cooped up in here?"

"Seemed better than the alternative." She modestly pulled the blanket up over her tank top.

"Which was...?" He'd grabbed some clothes from the closet and took them to the bathroom to change, but didn't close the door completely.

She watched him strip off his black T-shirt to reveal the rippled muscles beneath. Melanie stared. God, he had a beautiful body. Who knew beating a drum could produce that? Her cheeks burned, and she turned away.

"Getting more third degree from your sister," she said. "She's very interested in our history, especially how we met."

"I'll bet she is," he said, emerging from the bathroom with a fresh white tee and a pair of flannel pants. He sat at the edge of the bed. "So, basically, you're hiding."

"Yeah, I guess I'm hiding." Guilt stabbed at her. She should be doing her job, not lounging around in luxury. She could be doing more to make Gina dislike her, but there was only so much disapproval a person could take in a day. She braced for a lecture.

"Want some company?" He cocked his head and smiled.

"You aren't mad?"

He looked puzzled. "Why would I be mad? Frankly, I thought you'd beat it out of here the minute I left. I wouldn't blame you. Gina's a handful on a good day, but tonight"—he whistled—"she's in rare form tonight."

He watched the man and woman arguing silently on the screen. "*A Cigarette and a Glass?*"

"Yeah," she said, surprised. "You know your Samia Gamal movies."

"My mom used to watch them. I still have a box full of her videotapes somewhere in the garage. The old movies are good. I haven't seen them in years, but they aren't bad. I like the earlier ones a little more, when she was still with that guy—" He tapped his skull trying to think of a name.

"Farid Al Atrache?" she offered.

"Looks kinda like Desi Arnaz?"

"Yes! I like him, too," Melanie exclaimed then caught herself. This was all fake. They were not dating. Not. Dating. "I mean, those movies hold up, and the dancing is great. I used to watch them just for the dance scenes, but the stories have grown on me."

"I know what you mean," he said. "Mind if I join you over there?"

She realized she was taking up the whole bed. And all the pillows. She blushed and pulled a couple pillows off her stack and shifted to the side. "I guess not. It is our bed, right?"

He slid in beside her and positioned two pillows beneath his neck. "What's mine is yours, sweetheart. That's the deal until my sister leaves."

"Right," she said. She hated that she liked the sound of that. All of this—and all of him. "That's the deal," she repeated.

She settled back against the pillows again to watch the movie, but she could feel his eyes locked on her. She tried to ignore it, but when he didn't stop, she turned back to him. "Why are you staring at me?"

He smiled. "Sorry, I was just looking at your tattoo. I've never seen it up close. It's so intricate. Your ex does really good work."

She touched the lotus and thought of Chet. Had it really been just a couple weeks since they broke up? It felt like a lifetime ago. She hadn't thought of him in days, and she didn't want to think of him now.

"Thanks. It's my newest one, so the ink is still pretty fresh. This is my first one." She leaned over to show him her right shoulder. "I got it on my twenty-first birthday at that ink parlor that used to be next to the Newport Beach pier. It's gone now, but I used to love that place."

It all came back to her. The sand on the floor, the smell of the ocean wafting in the always-open front door, and the buzz of tattoo guns blazing wild art on bare skin. She sighed, remembering that first incredible experience. The adrenaline rush of being under that gun. The ecstasy of watching the image she had spent so much time doodling and perfecting on paper come alive on her arm. No other tattoo had ever felt quite the same since.

"Your first, huh? It must be special," he said.

She traced the hibiscus. It was her father's particular favorite. "It is special. For a lot of reasons."

They were the reasons she never talked about and tried never to even think about. She kept them to herself, chained to a concrete brick in the deepest, darkest parts of her memory.

But right now, with Taz so close and leaning in so intently, she could feel the chain loosening.

As she stared into his endlessly green eyes, she shivered, feeling naked and entirely exposed. But she knew she was safe. She could tell him about Dad, and about her dreams. She could tell him anything.

He flashed a sly grin as if he were reading her mind.

"Want to know one of my secrets?" he asked.

Her chest seized. Oh, God. Was he feeling it, too? "Uh, yeah," she said, trying to sound calm.

He turned back to the television. "I don't know. Maybe I shouldn't tell you."

"Hey, c'mon, that's not fair." She slapped him on the arm.

He was teasing. She could see it in the curl of his lips.

"You can't put something out there like that," she cajoled. "You have to tell me."

He cradled his arm like she'd really hurt him, but a smile spread widely across his face. "I can't tell you. If I do, you'll never want to leave this bed."

Her heart raced. She licked her lips and wondered when she'd last brushed her hair and whether her breath was fresh. "C'mon. Tell me."

"All right." He leaned over and pinned her against the pillow with his wide, strong chest. She gasped, breathing in his warm, woodsy scent.

He didn't seem to notice. He was pulling open a drawer of the nightstand.

Her mind raced. Was it what she thought it was? Was this really happening? Thank God she'd taken that bath.

When he leaned up, he presented her with a handful of candy packages. "Okay, you asked for it. Reese's Peanut Butter Cups, M&Ms, or Milky Way bar?"

Her shoulders sank. "Chocolate?"

He laughed like it was the funniest thing he'd heard all night. "Yeah. Pretty great, huh? It's like my own personal concession stand." He looked down at the two packages still in his hand. "You don't want one?"

She yanked the bag of M&Ms out of his grip and tore open a corner.

"Honestly, it's no wonder you're still single."

"Who's single?" he said and popped a whole chocolate cup into his mouth. "I have a girlfriend, remember?"

He laughed, jabbed her in the arm, and settled back to watch the rest of the movie.

CHAPTER TWENTY

THE NEXT MORNING, Melanie awoke to an empty bed.

Taz had nodded off almost immediately after the movie's credits ran. She hadn't had the heart to wake him and make him move to the fold-out bed.

She had just lain there most of the night, listening to him breathe, feeling the covers shift when he shifted. It was a peaceful sleep, but when she had awakened the next morning, he was already gone. The meeting with Garrett must have been an early one, she figured.

She, on the other hand, had nowhere to be. Silently, she thanked Deffner again for her glorious four-ten workweeks, which made every weekend a three-day weekend.

When she finally mustered the energy to get out of bed, sometime around nine in the morning, and passed the closed door of the guest room, she stopped to listen for signs of life within. Nothing. When she reached the kitchen, she realized why. Gina had left a handwritten note: *Taz, Going shopping for a costume then meeting a friend for dinner. Don't wait up.*

She had to hand it to the woman. She was determined. Nothing was going to keep her from the Pandemonium Ball. She wondered what kind of fireworks there'd be if Garrett didn't cough up the extra ticket.

CHAPTER TWENTY-ONE

LIKE GINA, MELANIE realized she had better get her costume, too.

She considered stopping by her mom's place to go through the boxes of performance costumes she'd stuffed in a storage shed in the carport.

They hadn't parted on the best terms, though. Another screaming match wasn't exactly the way she wanted to spend her day.

Instead, she headed for the dance studio.

"Looks like you've been busy," she said to Abby, who was sweeping the shop floor when she arrived.

The boutique had made significant progress since she'd last seen it. The shelves along the wall were full, the music corner was together, and the jewelry racks dripped with dangling, shiny things. There were just two empty, round racks sitting in the middle of the space beside an open box of hangers.

"It's coming together. Just need to figure out what moves from the shelves to the racks. The skirts, for sure. But I'm torn between the silk veils and the tribal belts for the other one."

"I vote belts. The tassels and fringe will look better hanging, don't you think?"

"Yeah, you're right. Belts it is." She moved to the shelf with three stacks of folded belts. She was turned away and was sorting through them when she added, "So?"

Melanie paused, confused. "So, what?"

Abby turned and planted her fists on her hips. "Really? You become Taz Roman's fake girlfriend, and then I don't hear from you again?"

"It's only been a couple of days."

"Two days, and I have no details. So spill it. What happened?"

Melanie shrugged. "It's fine. I'm staying at his place, and it's been fine."

Abby clipped the belt she was holding to a hanger and smirked. "You've fallen for him, haven't you? Miss Never In A Million Years has fallen for Taz Roman. I can't believe it."

"No, I haven't," Melanie snapped. "That's ridiculous." She craned her neck to look down the hallway.

"No one's here. Don't worry. Just me. Well, me and Taz Roman's new 'real' girlfriend."

"I'm not his girlfriend," Melanie cried. "His real girlfriend, anyway. Just a fake one, and that's it." If only she could keep the schoolgirl grin off her face.

Abby gave her a break, though, and went back to pulling the tasseled tribal belts off the shelf.

"Okay, so let's say there's nothing romantic going on. Is he at least holding up his end of the bargain? I figure since I haven't seen you that you must be practicing with him."

"Yeah, you wouldn't believe the dance room he has in his house. Actually, you wouldn't believe his house! I knew the Romans were, like, music royalty, but his house is a-ma-zing."

"So not a bad way to spend a few days, huh? When does his sister leave?"

"I don't know. Definitely not before the Pandemonium Ball, which reminds me. I have a huge favor to ask."

That got Abby's attention. "Taz invited me to go with him to the ball, but—"

"But you said, 'Only if I can bring my best friend, Abby'?"

Melanie chuckled. "I wish! You have no idea how much I wish you could be there, but he's only got one ticket."

Abby's eyes narrowed. "Just one, and he's taking you?"

Melanie nodded.

"Maybe Taz Roman has a little crush on you?"

"No way," Melanie scoffed, but she could feel her face burning. "That would never happen."

A little thought slipped through the crevices: Would it *never* happen? Was it really so far-fetched?

She shook it off.

"I was thinking about wearing one of the costumes we put together for the Marrakesh Nights performance a couple years ago, the black-and-white movie routine. Do you still have those?"

"I'm sure I do. I put all that stuff in the back room. I'll go check."

"No, I can do it."

"Are you sure?"

"Yeah, of course," she said. "You have plenty to do." It was the truth. Abby needed to focus on the boutique, not making sure Melanie had a proper costume.

But Melanie also couldn't stop thinking about what Abby had said. Could there be something more to Taz's invitation? The prospect thrilled her, and she had to fight back the goofy grin aching to give her away. If Abby spotted it, Melanie would never hear the end of it.

What she needed was a good, long search in the storeroom to get her mind back on track. She needed to bring these irrational thoughts back to the real world and forget these ridiculous ideas about Taz.

CHAPTER TWENTY-TWO

WHEN MELANIE RETURNED to Taz's place that evening, she found him in the kitchen, hunched over a bowl of red pepper soup.

"Oh, it's just you," he said when he saw her and went back eating.

"Well, hello to you, too," she replied sharply.

"Sorry," he said. "I thought you were Gina."

"Nope, just me. I don't suppose you have any more of that soup left, do you?"

Her stomach rumbled. It had been hours since she'd eaten the burger she'd bought in a drive-through before visiting the studio.

"Help yourself," he said, motioning with his head at the pan on the stove.

She grabbed a bowl—finding the correct cabinet on the third try—and ladled herself a healthy portion.

She sat across from him at the kitchen island and dug in.

"I got a costume," she said after a bite.

"Really? What is it?"

She wiggled her finger until she swallowed her bite. "Not telling. I want it to be a surprise."

His eyes widened. "Should I be scared? I see what some of you women wear to that thing, or maybe I should say *don't wear*."

"You wish. No, it's nothing like that. I just want it to be a surprise."

"Okay," he said, still wary. "I wonder what Gina will come up with. With her, it's always the bigger, the better. One year she went as *The Secret Garden*, with vines and fake flowers. The works. She hired a Hollywood special-effects artist to make the headdress. It was extravagant."

Suddenly Melanie wasn't feeling so confident about her own choice. "Sounds pretty spectacular. So I guess you were able to get a ticket for her?" *Please no, please no.*

"Yeah, it actually wasn't a big deal. I just didn't want her to go. Now I'm stuck. Oh wait, *we're* stuck."

"Right." She cracked a half-hearted smile.

He watched her for a moment then said, "I have to admit. You continue to surprise me.

Her stomach flip-flopped. "Really, why?"

"I can't imagine a few audition tips make it worth what you went through last night."

Was he really concerned about her? Maybe she'd misjudged him.

"It wasn't so bad," she said.

He shook his head. "Well, I owe you big time. I know that."

The nerves in her gut calmed. "I know how you can make it up to me." It might have given her hives to say something like that to him a few days ago, but not now.

He perked up, amused. "Really?"

She took her empty soup bowl to the sink, rinsed it, and placed it in the empty dishwasher. After she'd stalled long enough, she turned back with a wicked grin and said, "Give me five minutes, then meet me in the dance room."

CHAPTER TWENTY-THREE

TAZ WAS ALREADY in the dance room, waiting when Melanie walked in wearing her usual practice outfit—black leggings, a snug crop top, and a hip scarf with dangling gold coins that swished and jangled when she moved.

"You look ready to dance," he said.

"Are you ready to coach?"

He laughed. "I suppose we'll see, won't we?"

"I suppose we will."

She went to the stereo, plugged in her smartphone, and selected the song. When the slow, flute-like melody filled the speakers, she turned back to him.

"This is what I'm planning to use at the audition. What do you think?"

He listened. When the solo flute gave way to a synthesized electronic beat, he nodded.

"Nice choice. Good mix of traditional and modern beats. How about showing me what you're going to do with it."

Her lips quirked in an "I accept your challenge" grin. She went back to her smartphone and restarted the song. She moved to the center of the room as the flute's sinewy melody began.

As she stood there, a flash of fear washed over her. What if he hated the routine? What if he was just too nice to say she didn't have a chance in hell at this audition?

"Relax," he said calmly from the bench alongside the wall, as though he could read her thoughts.

Ordinarily, someone pointing out that she was tense only made her more tense. He didn't. Instead, his words calmed her. They were comforting, like a warm, fuzzy blanket.

She shut her eyes, took a deep breath, and let the music guide her. She had danced through this routine so many times, so many hundreds, maybe thousands of times, that she didn't have to think about it. Her arms, her feet, every part of her knew what to do without a thought, as if she were just a passenger floating on a beautiful cloud of music.

Since their last session, she had worked to incorporate his suggestions. She held back and took her time. Instead of pushing the music, she let the music pull her through the moves.

Too soon it seemed, the song ended, and she was standing in her final pose, feeling as if she were waking up from a dream.

She glanced at Taz, hopeful, eager. "What do you think? Is it better?"

He tilted his head, as though he were mulling the question. For an instant, the old fear returned. He hated it. Obviously he hated it.

Then he smiled that sweet, toothy celebrity smile. The smile that melted her self-doubt.

"It was good," he said. "Really good. You aren't rushing anymore. Big improvement."

The weight of a hundred-pound stone seemed to lift from her shoulders. An unabashed, goofy grin spread across her face.

Then she noticed his smile faltered. He'd crossed one leg, letting his foot dangle over the other knee, and it was bouncing. It didn't take a body language expert to see he was holding something back.

"Okay," she said. "There's more. What is it?" She tried to keep the disappointment out of her voice. She tried to sound like she didn't care.

He stiffened.

"It's a super-minor thing. I probably shouldn't even mention it."

He didn't want to hurt her feelings. She could see that, and maybe that was what made her feel worse.

"Just be honest. You hated it."

"I did not hate it. I just think…" He held his jaw and mulled his next words.

She wanted to scream.

"Just say it," she demanded.

"Okay," he said finally. "It's the way you look."

She took a step back. She certainly hadn't expected that. "I already told you, the tattoos are part of who I am. If people don't like it—"

"No," he said, "that's not what I mean. What I mean is the way you look at the audience, or rather how you don't look at the audience."

What the hell did that mean?

The look on her face must have said exactly that, because he stood up and tried again. "In my experience, a great performance is when there's a balance between the dancer giving her energy to the audience and taking their energy into herself. A yin and yang, an ebb and a flow."

It sort of made sense, but what did that mean for her routine?

"It's the dancer dancing for the audience," he continued, "and then dancing for herself. Now that I'm thinking about it and trying to put my finger on it, I think it boils down to eye contact. You don't make any."

"I do," she said with a huff.

He shook his head. "You look down, or up, or at your arms, or your feet. But you don't connect with anyone in the audience."

"That's not true," she said, but an annoying little voice inside was telling her he was right.

"Then prove me wrong. Dance it again, and look at me." He sank back on the bench, crossed his arms, and challenged her again.

"Fine." *He thinks he's so smart.*

She restarted the music and took her place in the center of the room.

He *was* wrong. She was sure of it. Silently, she repeated: *eye contact, eye contact, eye contact.*

When she danced, she tried to force herself to look at him, but those deep-forest green eyes, those impossibly green eyes, made her feel so strange, and so disoriented. She missed a step, and alarms went off in her head. Her breath came quick and labored.

This was a disaster. How ridiculous she must look, with her glance ricocheting off the walls like a rubber bullet.

She caught his smile, and he said, "You're doing great."

The words felt like a warm embrace. The tension that had accumulated in her shoulders and knees vanished. She could breathe.

"Yeah," he said, nodding. "That's so much better. Here, when you get to the part where you tip your head…" He jumped up and joined her on the dance floor. "Instead of holding your head straight-on this way, tilt it, just a bit, like this."

The palms of his hands were holding her cheeks and gently he guided her head to the side.

He was so close, she could smell the soft, woodsy scent of him. Feel the tenderness of his touch. She stared at his neck, memorizing the dip of his collarbone, the line of his jaw. It was intoxicating, this feeling. Like there was no one else in the world.

Wait, this was crazy. This was Taz. This meant nothing. She tried to shake it off.

He pulled his hands away.

"I'm sorry, did I hurt you?"

She glanced up and saw those pools of green again, and she was lost.

"No, I'm fine, I just…" She couldn't continue. Her heart was racing. Her glance slid to his rosy-pink lips. Those full, infuriatingly sexy lips.

She opened her mouth to try again, but before she could utter a word, his lips were on hers. Hot and demanding. Insistent. She returned their fervor with her own.

She wound her arms around him, clutching the hard muscles that ran the length of his back, crushing away the space between them. His chest against hers, his hips pressing into hers.

It was insanity, feeling him against her, his lips sliding down her neck, his breath making her tingle in so many amazing places.

When he grabbed her ass, gripping her and pressing her against that incredibly hard part of him, she gasped. God, this should stop. She should pull away. She knew she should push him away, but even as the thought emerged, she already knew she couldn't. She wanted this. She'd wanted it for a long time.

He pulled back, and she opened her eyes. Those gorgeous green eyes of his were staring at her, searching her expression, looking so damn vulnerable and adorable it made her knees weak.

"Should I stop?" he breathed, his voice rough, his breath labored.

Her own breath caught in her throat. She should say yes. She knew it. It was the practical thing to do. But she couldn't pull away.

She whispered, "Don't you dare."

CHAPTER TWENTY-FOUR

THAT WAS THE only permission Taz needed. In an instant, he scooped her up, wrapping his arms around the soft curves of her hips, and she responded by wrapping her legs—those gorgeously strong and supple legs—around his hips.

Damn, he wanted her. It almost frightened him how much he wanted her. He couldn't lie, it wasn't as if he hadn't thought of this moment. There'd been plenty of times his thoughts had drifted to her—wondering what it would feel like to run his fingers through her loose, honey-brown hair, or let his hands roam over those gorgeously full breasts. The cropped tee she had on had nearly undone him, fitting so snugly, so perfectly around that part of her anatomy. He could practically make out the lace pattern of her bra. God, this was crazy.

What his body was telling him to do was slam her against the wall, rip away that tee and those leggings, and take her right here. It almost surprised him that it was his own conscience that stopped him. Not because his grandmother stared down at him from the wall, but because it felt different this time.

She was different.

She didn't adore him or fawn over him or make a fuss like so many other women did. Hell, sometimes she didn't even seem to like him. At least not at first. But when she smiled or when she said something kind, he knew she meant it. He knew she had no ulterior motives.

In some strange, inexplicable way, he knew he could trust her in a way he hadn't trusted a woman in a long time.

Tonight when he'd seen her on the dance floor, he couldn't help but remember how it had felt to be with her onstage. How perfectly in tune they'd been and how much he had wanted her that very first night.

Then, like now, there were so many reasons to hold back, to keep their relationship uncomplicated. To make sure things stayed on track, at least until Gina was safely on her way back to New York.

There were so many good, solid reasons. He just couldn't remember them right now. All he could think of was the soft lavender smell of her skin, the warm citrus scent of her hair, the velvety feel of her arms and her back, and the strength in her kiss.

Before he even knew what he meant to do, he was carrying her out of the dance room, down the hall, and directly to his room. Their room.

She didn't protest. When he dropped her onto the deep, pillowy comforter, she looked around and smiled.

That genuine, sweet smile of hers. Whatever strength he had left was gone. Whatever second thoughts he had vanished. He lowered himself on top of her and wrapped his arms around her, feeling every part of himself touch her.

None of this could be wrong, he told himself, because it felt too damn right.

CHAPTER TWENTY-FIVE

THE NEXT MORNING, Melanie awakened to the rustling of sheets beside her. The memories of the night before flooded back. All the kisses and caresses. All the ways he had stroked her body and slowly driven her wild with desire. It had seemed an eternity before he took her, and only then—she remembered with a blush—it had been because she had rolled on top of him and taken matters into her own hands.

A bold move, but she recalled he hadn't seemed to mind. She pressed her face into the soft, down pillow to hide the grin spreading across her face.

Behind her, she could hear Taz roll out of bed, pad to the bathroom, and close the door. Morning light glowed around the edges of the lush draperies, and she knew she should get up, but it all seemed so perfect right now. The sexed feeling gave her a warm glow, and she didn't want to lose it.

She wanted to linger in the memory of that amazing night.

When Taz emerged from the shower, with just a towel around his waist, she was propped up in bed, watching a rerun of *Supernatural.*

"That's a first," he said, using a second towel to rub his wet hair.

"What?" Her mind raced with possibilities. First woman in his bed? No way. First morning-after? Just as unlikely.

"First time I've seen you watch anything in color."

She laughed. "I'm not narrow-minded. I watch a lot of different things."

He walked over to the bed and crawled toward her, nuzzling her neck with kisses. "You are definitely not narrow-minded. Some of the things you did last night, *whew!* They blew my mind."

"Me? I remember a few... shall we say adventurous... moments on your part as well."

He pulled back, and with a self-satisfied grin, added, "You're right, I was on fire last night."

She slapped him lightly. "You're naughty."

He caught her hand and pulled her closer. He looked at her and quirked his eyebrow. "I know. It makes us a pretty good pair, doesn't it?"

He planted a long, delicious kiss on her lips before she could say anything. Then he pulled back, rose, and turned. She was going to make her comeback when he let the white towel drop to the floor, and he walked away in all his glorious nakedness. She stared at the way his backside begged to be touched, the way the muscles of his back rippled. The words vanished.

When he reached the closet door and opened it, he glanced over his shoulder. "You aren't looking at my ass, are you?"

She turned at least fifty shades of red because he knew as well as she did that was exactly what she was doing.

"I plead the fifth," she said and, with the sheet wrapped around herself, she rushed into the bathroom to claim it for herself.

"Aw, c'mon," he said as she closed the door. "I showed you mine. The least you could do is return the favor."

It should have added to her embarrassment, but all she could do was grin.

CHAPTER TWENTY-SIX

BY THE TIME Melanie had dressed, dried her hair, and headed down to the kitchen to find something to eat, the smell of freshly brewed coffee wafted through the house. She followed it like a bee to pollen.

Taz was sitting at the center island, finishing a plate of toast slathered with butter and strawberry jam.

"Morning, sunshine," he said when he saw her.

She craned her neck around, looking to see if they were alone.

"Don't worry. The she-wolf isn't around. She's off doing God-knows-what."

Melanie breathed easier. So it would be just the two of them for a little while longer. Perfect.

"There's practically a full pot in there for you." He took the last bite of toast and deposited his plate in the sink. She saw his coffee was loaded in a travel mug.

"You going somewhere?" she asked.

"Yeah, Garrett wants to do a sound check at the hotel before the party preppers go crazy."

The party. Damn, with all that had happened last night, she'd forgotten about the Pandemonium Ball.

"Cool," she said. "I have a lot to do, too."

"Well, I think you'll have the place to yourself. Gina said she'll meet us there."

A welcome relief.

"So are you going to give me at least a hint about your costume?"

She smiled deviously. "No way! But I think you'll like it."

"That certainly whets the appetite." He wiggled his eyebrows. "I'll be back about four to pick you up. Think you'll be ready?"

"I'll be ready."

He bent to peck her lips then paused and instead planted a longer, deeper kiss that made her toes curl. "Bye," he said and walked out the door.

"Bye," she whispered to his back and waited until she heard the front door shut to do her victory dance.

CHAPTER TWENTY-SEVEN

THE REST OF Melanie's day was spent in a wonderful, leisurely fog. She practiced until every limb ached then climbed into bed for a nap with Spike cradled beside her. When she awoke, she slipped into a long, hot bath. And the whole time, her mind kept drifting back to the wonderful night before.

She should probably call Abby and confess she'd been right. But there was plenty of time for that. Right now it was fun having this wonderful thing all to herself. Just for a little while longer.

By the time Taz returned at four, she was waiting in the living room, standing at the back window that looked out toward the Pacific.

She waited for him to look up from the mail he was thumbing through before she said hello. When his eyes caught hers and widened, she let a slow, sexy smile creep across her face. This was the reaction she'd been hoping for.

Without a word, she glided forward in long, stage-worthy strides, lifting her arms to make the drape of white chiffon attached to her upper arms and wrists billow and flutter against the matching circle skirt. She dipped and spun, letting him take in her whole appearance: the vintage-styled hair, the smoky makeup, the bra and belt, thick with sequins and jewels that shone like polished onyx. She pressed up against him, her lips coming to rest just beneath his.

"So, what do you think?"

"You look like you stepped out of one of those Samia Gamal movies."

She pumped her fist in victory. "Yes! I knew you'd get it." She twisted and fluttered her arms. "The chiffon is straight out of *The Glass and the Cigarette,* but the rest is my own tribal touch." She brushed her hand lightly over the bits of embroidered glass called *shisha*, the cowrie shells, tiny tassels, and assorted bits of chunky Bedouin jewelry covering her bra and belt, and her headband—all black, gray, and white to give the illusion she was an image captured on the silver screen.

"I like it," he whispered, his voice rough.

He raised his hands to her hips and bent his head to kiss her, but she slipped out of reach before he could.

"Hey," he said with a frown.

"Sorry," she said. "The makeup is pretty sturdy, but it'll smudge if I'm not careful. Actually, I need your help with my back." It had taken nearly an hour to get the application just right to cover her natural skin color. She'd had to use extra to cover her tattoos.

She'd managed a nice blend on all the parts of herself she could see and reach, but there was a patch between her shoulder blades she couldn't get to. She grabbed the bottle of light gray from the table, handed it to him with a small sponge, and turned her back to him.

"So this is all I get to touch, all night?"

"Mmm-hmm."

"That's not fair, you know."

"Last time I checked, life wasn't fair. Please try to blend it evenly, if you can. It's a little tricky."

In a moment she felt the cool touch of the paint on her skin and his fingers brushing in slow, smooth strokes.

"What's with the goosebumps?" he said softly. He was so close she could feel his breath on her neck.

"How do you do that?"

"What?"

"Make lathering on skin paint sexy."

"I guess it's a gift."

She smiled and resisted the temptation to break her own no-touching rule.

"Okay, looks good," he said. He pulled his hand away, and she felt the absence suddenly, like a splash of cold water.

In fact, a cold shower was exactly what she needed to get herself composed again. Since that wasn't in the cards, she'd have to make do with the time it took him to get changed to get herself together.

"Are you ready to go?" he asked and picked up his keys.

She frowned. "Didn't you forget something?"

He shook his head.

"Your costume?" she pressed. "You haven't changed yet."

"Oh, that," he said. He reached into his back pocket and pulled out a mask. It was covered in black satin and shaped to cover half his face. He slid it over his head, and with his white tunic, he looked like a reverse *Phantom of the Opera*. He spread out his arms. "Ta-da!"

"You're kidding me," she said.

"What, you don't like it?"

"It's not that. You look good. It's just not fair. This"—she gestured around herself—"took hours. That took you two seconds."

He smirked devilishly. "Funny, last time I checked, life wasn't fair."

CHAPTER TWENTY-EIGHT

MELANIE HAD TO admit, driving to downtown Los Angeles in Taz's Porsche was nothing like driving up in her old Honda. Not only did people slow down and make room in the lane when Taz put on his blinker, instead of speeding up and riding the bumper of the vehicle in front of them as they usually did, but they also smiled. The tipped their chins with respect as he passed. They were friendly.

The best part was pulling up to The Victorian Hotel, an older but still regal building in LA's downtown district. The valet parking attendant didn't grudgingly approach the car. The guy actually jogged over to open her door and offer a hand.

"Welcome to The Victorian, miss. Are you here for the ball?"

"We are," she answered, trying to stifle the grin burning inside her.

"If there's anything we can do to make your visit more enjoyable, please don't hesitate to ask."

"Thank you," she said as she stood a little straighter and a little prouder. So this is what it was like for the other half? Not bad.

"Looks like we aren't too early." Taz dipped his head toward the costumed crowd lingering near the entrance. He came up to her and slipped his hand around to the small of her back and rested it on her belt.

The simple gesture gave her tingles all over again. It surprised her how natural it felt. She stared at her gray arms, her gray, bare midriff. Damn, body paint. She wanted to nuzzle against him, to feel the warmth of him, but she couldn't without ruining all her hard work.

"You look fantastic, by the way," he whispered in her ear. "Did I already tell you that?"

"You did, but don't let that stop you."

"That's my girl."

There it was again. That lush, warm sensation radiating through her.

"C'mon," he said. "Let's check out the party."

A liveried doorman swung open the brass-and-glass door for them, and Melanie nearly gasped. The lobby would have been right at home in a European palace. It was exquisite, with all its marble, polished wood, and shiny brass.

Still, the hotel paled in comparison to the crowd. As they made their way through the lobby, they passed a sea of wild characters. It was like a Tim Burton film collided with an Anne Rice novel, with touches of *Lord of the Rings* and *Star Wars*. She slowed to avoid stepping on a woman's train assembled entirely of peacock feathers and jostled out of the way of a woodland nymph carrying two plastic cups filled with a neon-blue liquor and glowing swizzle sticks.

"Love the costume. Silver screen. Very cool," the nymph whispered as she passed.

"Thanks," Melanie said.

Taz bypassed the line where new arrivals were checking in and found a table where a single person sat with a sign reading Talent Check-In. He stepped up and handed over a card.

The young man, dressed like he was on his way to a Renaissance faire, handed back two purple wristbands. "All-access. Have fun."

"We intend to, thanks," Taz said. He put one on Melanie's wrist and then his own.

"So we're official now?" she asked.

"We're official." He winked. "C'mon, you're going to love this." He opened the door to the ballroom.

The music that had been thumping through the walls spilled out like a tsunami, a bass-heavy electronic beat that penetrated every move and thought. It was impossible not to bob or sway, and in her mind she was already dancing to its rhythm.

But Taz was on the move. He put his hand on the back of her belt again and guided her deeper into the darkened ballroom, where candelabras flickered with LED flames and bright electric colors chased each other over the crowd.

He was heading toward the long bar when he leaned down and said over the cacophony of music and voices, "I see Garrett. I'll introduce you."

She stared at a woman walking by who was dressed in a shimmering, barely-there toga and wearing a headdress like a golden silk starfish on her head. Amazing.

"Did you hear me?"

"Yeah," she said. "That's great." The way she was feeling, she would have said yes to anything. It was intoxicating being here, like she'd fallen down Alice's rabbit hole and found herself in some kind of make-believe world. It was like a dream, like a big, wonderful dream she never wanted to leave.

She followed behind Taz, watching the parade of beautiful freaks, smiling at the medieval knight and lady cheetah, the Willy Wonka lookalike and the warrior princess. When they stopped in front of a man whose only remarkable quality was his impossible likeness to a young David Bowie, she nearly laughed.

Taz clasped the man around the shoulders and gave him a brotherly embrace.

"Garrett, this is the friend I was telling you about. This is Melanie."

Garrett reached out and took her hand. "It's a pleasure to meet you, Melanie," he said, his crisp British accent giving the words a stoic formality. "I understand we'll be seeing you at the audition."

Her giddiness vanished, and the importance of the meeting hit her like a concrete block. "Yes, you will. I'm, uh, I'm really looking forward to it."

Oh, God. Could she be any lamer?

"It's refreshing to see someone so confident," he said and glanced at Taz.

"She has every reason to be confident," Taz piped in. "She's good. Really good."

Wow, did he really think so? He'd never told her that. She was about to thank him when a trio of young women approached, dressed as tribal belly-dancing fairies. Melanie recognized them all as Belly Dance Divas who had performed at the Shimmy Shop's fund-raising showcase last month.

"Hey, boss," said the blonde with opalescent wings. "I seem to remember there was a promise of drinks being on you tonight. Do you remember that, girls?"

The other two nodded their agreement. "I remember that," one said. "Me, too," said the other.

"Whoa," Garrett said, chuckling. "You're not ganging up on me, are you?"

"Not at all," the blonde said with a haughty smile. "We're just thirsty."

"All right. I suppose a promise is a promise." He turned to Taz and Melanie. "Apparently the next round is on me, but I shall need an extra pair of hands. Care to help, Taz? Leave these dancers to their evil schemes?"

"Yes, run along and help, Taz," the blonde said mischievously. "We'll keep your friend company."

Taz gave Melanie a concerned look that didn't escape the blonde's notice.

"Don't worry, Taz. We won't scare her away."

He didn't look convinced. Melanie suddenly wondered if Taz the Romancer had a history with one of these Divas. Hell, maybe all of them, if the rumors were true. Still, it was amusing watching him squirm, and the taunting seemed too playful to be malicious.

"Yeah," she said, reassuringly. "Go on. I'm feeling thirsty, too. You don't mind, do you?"

"All right," he said. "But don't run off. We'll be right back."

CHAPTER TWENTY-NINE

WHEN THE MEN were gone, the blonde turned to Melanie. "I remember you from the Shimmy Shop's benefit show. That was a fantastic night. I don't think we were ever properly introduced, though. I'm Tilly, this is Gwen"—she pointed to the brunette on her right—"and this is Lindsay."

"Of course," Melanie said. "It's great to see you again. The shop is doing much better. The classes are filling up, and the boutique should open any day now. It's been really great, and Abby owes a lot of that to you guys."

"It was so fun," Tilly said. "We loved doing it. There were so many talented dancers there. Like you! Your piece was amazing. You know the Divas are holding auditions next weekend, don't you? Have you ever considered trying out?"

She turned back to the others, who were nodding and smiling in agreement.

Melanie, who wasn't usually at a loss for words, stood mute. Was this really happening? Was she going to wake up at any moment and find herself drooling on her pillow in her mother's guest room?

"I've thought about it," she managed to say before she felt the urge to giggle. Good grief, she couldn't do that in front of Belly Dance Divas.

"Definitely think about it," the one named Lindsay said. "Love your costume, by the way. It looks kind of familiar, but I can't place it."

Melanie was about to explain the inspiration when two women approached the group.

"I'm so sorry to intrude," said one with a familiar Southern drawl, "but are you guys the Belly Dance Divas?"

The women were dressed like space-age saloon girls, with their sexy silver lamé corsets and bustles, and they were covered head to toe in bluish-green body makeup that shimmered in the light.

Melanie scrutinized their faces, but they didn't register. Under all that blue paint, they could be anybody.

"We are," Tilly said.

The one who spoke turned to her friend and gushed, "I told you it was them!" She turned back to Tilly. "Would it be okay if we took a picture with you for our blog?"

Then it all came back. The drawl and the wild blond hair she'd only glimpsed. These were the bloggers she'd overheard in the ladies' room at the Sultan's Tent.

"Of course," Tilly said. "Do you want all of us?"

"Absolutely, if you guys don't mind," the woman said. She turned to her friend. "Let's get someone to take the picture."

Melanie put her hand up and said, "I'll take it."

Tilly tapped her hand back down. "No way. You've got to be in the picture, too."

"But I'm not a Diva," she whispered to Tilly.

She whispered back, "Maybe not yet, but soon enough, right?"

It didn't matter, though, because the one with the camera had handed it off to a guy who looked like the Big Bad Wolf in gladiator garb.

The women pulled together, the gladiator wolf said, "Say, 'cheesy pizza,'" they all said "cheesy pizza,'" and he snapped a few pictures.

He handed the camera back to one of the women, and they both went around the group shaking hands and thanking the Divas.

When the blonde got to Melanie, she paused mid-shake. Melanie froze.

"Hey, I remember you. Didn't you dance at the Sultan's Tent last week?"

Was that a frown?

"Yeah, I was there," Melanie answered cautiously. Which way was this conversation headed?

"We didn't expect a dancer to be there," the blonde said, quickly recovering her smile. "It was quite a show."

"Thank you," Melanie said, relieved. "It's nice of you to say so."

The woman leaned in. "So, are you—"

"Shelley, c'mon."

The woman's friend was tugging at her arm.

"There's a chocolate fountain in the banquet room," the shorter one said. "You know how much I love those. C'mon, let's go."

The blonde turned, and something unspoken passed between them in glances. Then she turned back with a plastered on smile. "We should go, but I do hope we can chat more later." With that, her friend led her into the crowd.

Melanie smiled. Her first fan. Was it possible for the night to get any better?

CHAPTER THIRTY

"SO WHAT DO you think?" Taz asked as he and Garrett stood on the fringe of the crowded bar, his fingers tapping on his thigh.

"About what?" Garrett said in that too-casual tone that meant he knew exactly what.

"About Melanie. There's something about her, don't you think? Something kinda special."

Garrett scrutinized him a moment then said, "I should have known. I thought you were getting cold feet about the tour, or maybe something about that legacy project of yours. But it's just the usual thing. Just another girl who has you in thrall."

Taz made a face. "She doesn't have me *in thrall*, or in anything else. I just think she might be a good fit for the troupe."

"Really? I am sure that assessment has nothing to do with the fact that you're shagging her?"

"No!"

Garrett tugged at the sleeves of his blue-velvet jacket. "No, it isn't the reason, or no, you aren't sleeping with her?"

Taz scoffed. "Neither," he said, hoping the flush on his cheeks didn't tell Garrett the truth. He kept his eyes on the bartender. At the first glimmer of eye contact, he hailed him. "We'd like to order," he demanded, a little too forcefully.

When the bartender slipped away to retrieve their drinks, Garrett turned back to him.

"So I can count on you for the tour? You aren't backing out? I can't be looking for a replacement at the last minute."

"What the hell? I miss a couple meetings, and you're talking about a replacement?"

"Of course I am. This is going to be the biggest tour we've ever staged. We've already booked twenty-five cities on four continents, and there are more to come. There are a lot of moving parts now. I can't change things at a moment's notice, not like last time."

Last time. He was still holding on to that old history. "That was a long time ago, before there ever was a Belly Dance Divas. Everything worked out. I thought we agreed on that."

"Yes, it worked out last time. I just don't want there to be a next time. I don't want any surprises. I've wagered everything on this tour."

The bartender returned with six martini glasses filled with an impossibly bright-green liquid and topped by an orange twist. Garrett paid and tipped—generously, as usual.

"Look," Taz said, taking up half the glasses, "all I'm saying is, check her out when she auditions. I think you'll like what you see."

Garrett stuffed his wallet in his breast pocket and took up the rest of the drinks. "Fine," he said as they walked back. "I get it. Does she?"

"What do you mean?"

Garrett answered with a shrug, and then it was too late. They were already back at the group, and he was back in gracious-host mode.

"All right, ladies," Garrett said, "your bribes—I mean, your drinks, are here. I think you'll like these. They're called Sonic Screwdrivers." He distributed the glasses, and Taz did the same.

He leaned over to Melanie. "These were Garrett's idea. I don't know what's in them, but if you hate it, I'll get you something else."

She wrinkled her nose then shrugged. "I don't know. Looks kind of interesting." She sipped and nodded. "Actually, it's good."

He sipped his own. An orange-flavored liqueur, something slightly fizzy. She was right. It wasn't half bad. He leaned closer to her. "So what do you think about all this? I know it's a lot to take in."

She sipped again then gazed around. "I think it's incredible. No wonder people say it's the best party of the year. I just hope I fit in."

"You don't have to worry about that. You fit in just fine." He leaned closer, and she leaned in too.

Every part of him wanted to be near her, to touch her. If only there wasn't all that damn makeup in the way. But her lips were so close. Maybe just a kiss…

A hand on his back stopped the thought. He turned to find long, perfectly manicured fingernails painted cherry red.

"There you are, darling," a husky, feminine voice said. "I've been looking everywhere for you."

CHAPTER THIRTY-ONE

MELANIE PEEKED AROUND Taz to see a woman who looked like Elvira dressed in a slinky scarlet-red gown and petting the long black hair draped around her generously exposed breasts. She smirked. "I didn't think I was ever going to find you two."

Taz frowned, and his eyebrows knit together.

The woman stamped a foot and held out her arms. "Don't you recognize your own sister?"

Great. Gina and her rotten timing.

She held out her arms and spun around like a fashion model. "Do you like it? I found a seamstress on Melrose who whipped it up in just four hours. It was amazing, like something out of *Project Runway*. But do you know the best part? She has a friend who does monster makeup for the movies. She came in and did all of this." She fanned her red-lacquered fingernails around her face and the ample décolletage that was not quite falling out of the deep V neckline that ended somewhere near her navel.

"It looks great, Gina," Taz said with the kind of hesitation you would expect from a brother concerned that his sister was revealing so much skin, even if it was covered in ghostly movie makeup.

If Gina noticed, it didn't show in the way she beamed. Then her gaze settled on Melanie, and the smile disappeared.

"And what are you supposed to be? The Ghost of Belly Dance Past?" She laughed like it was the funniest joke in the world.

Melanie forced herself to chuckle and curled her fingers into fists so she didn't throttle the woman's throat.

"Oh, but I'm being so rude," Gina announced. "You have to forgive me. Look who I brought with me."

She turned and grabbed the hand of a tall and willowy woman dressed in an elaborate headdress of wildfowl feathers and an equally plumed bra and miniskirt, chatting with the wolf gladiator beside them.

"Tamara worked her magic, got herself an invite, and jumped on a plane this morning when she heard I'd be all by my lonesome tonight. That's just the sweetest thing ever. Don't you think so, Taz?"

By the look on his face, he did not think so. He looked like someone had socked him in the gut. Melanie didn't have a chance to ask why, because the Belly Dance Divas and Garrett were making awkward shifting noises behind her. When she turned, Tilly leaned forward. "It's probably best if we leave. This could get—" She made a tortured face. "We'll catch up with you later."

Before Melanie could protest, they were gone, disappearing into the crowd.

Melanie stood, stunned. What was happening? Who was this woman?

Taz was still staring at Tamara, but his expression had changed from bewildered to hurt.

Gina, on the other hand, looked like she'd just scored the match point.

"What am I missing here?" Melanie blurted. "What's going on?"

Gina swooped over, took her arm, and started leading her toward the bar. "We should probably give Taz and Tamara a moment. They haven't seen each other in so long, I'm sure they have a lot of catching up to do."

Melanie glanced frantically at Taz. Did *he* want her to leave? He wasn't saying yes, but he wasn't saying no, either. He was just staring at Tamara.

"C'mon, Melanie," Gina cooed. "Let's see what's happening in the other rooms."

Melanie didn't care what was happening anywhere else. She wanted to know what was happening right here, right now, because none of this was making sense. Who was this woman standing beside him with that coy smile?

Then it hit her.

This was his ex-fiancée. The woman who had trampled on his heart.

Melanie flashed another questioning glance at Taz, all but begging him to ask her to stay.

He didn't. He didn't say a thing.

Okay. That was her answer. She turned back to Gina, her jaw set, every muscle tense. "Yeah," she said, "let's go."

CHAPTER THIRTY-TWO

MELANIE WALKED BESIDE Gina toward the bar, but her mind was still on Taz. Why hadn't he said anything? He hadn't even introduced her.

Why wouldn't he even introduce her?

Maybe it was obvious.

She was a fool. Of course she'd fallen for him, just as Abby had warned. She'd thought she was so immune, so superior to all the other women who had fallen for him, and here she was, one of the many. She was just another notch.

The pain in her heart became anger—a cruel, raw animal that clawed away the fantasy she'd been living in this past week.

To think, she actually thought Taz cared about her. That he might be falling for her. What an idiot.

She tipped back the drink she'd been trying so carefully not to spill, drained the last of it then planted the empty martini glass on the bar.

"Another, please," she declared to the bartender and turned to Gina. "You're buying, right?"

Amusement crossed the woman's face. "I guess I am." She ordered herself a chardonnay and pulled a few bills from her cherry-red clutch.

Melanie glanced back at Taz. He was still standing with Tamara, one hand on his hip, the other fidgeting at his side. She seemed to be doing the talking, but he must have been listening, because he wasn't doing anything else. He certainly wasn't looking for Melanie.

If he was going to treat her like trash, she wasn't going to make it easy for him. She took a good, long gulp of her new atomic-green drink, and turned to Gina. "I think they've had enough time to catch up."

She didn't wait for an answer. Just tightened her grip on her drink and marched back to Taz.

She was so focused on Taz and his ex that she almost didn't notice the furry, sandal-strapped foot that stepped in front of her. "Hey, gorgeous," the gladiator wolf said.

Melanie looked behind her for Gina.

"You're about the sexiest ghost I've ever seen."

Melanie rolled her eyes. Really? This was his pickup line? "I'm not a ghost, Big, Bad, whatever you are. If you don't mind, I have to get back to my—" She stopped. She was about to say "boyfriend," but he certainly wasn't that. "Forget it," she said and walked away.

What she should have said was "fake boyfriend." Because that's what he was, right? He was fake. All of it had been fake. Every minute of it. She took another drink and hoped it would dampen the pain.

"So did I miss anything?" she snapped, her voice almost steady, when she plopped herself in the middle of their conversation. Now she had a plan. She'd show him the past week didn't mean anything to her, either. She downed another long gulp and let it burn its electric-green courage into her. She was already feeling better. A bit dizzy, but better.

Now Taz was looking at her. His eyes narrowed. "Are you drunk?"

"No," she said but found herself stumbling two steps backward. He grabbed her free arm to steady her and took the nearly empty glass from the other.

"Hey, you can't do that," she said and tried to grab it back but missed. "It's not like you're my boyfriend, you know."

That got a reaction from him. Maybe it was surprise, maybe it was anger. Who cared? At least he was looking at her, paying attention to *her*, not this Fowl-Faced Barbie doll.

"Be careful," he said, his voice low and menacing.

"Be careful about what? Telling your sister that this whole thing is a huge lie? Telling her we're only pretending to live together so you can keep her off your back? Who would ever believe we'd be a couple? Hell, we don't even know each other, right?"

"What did you say?"

The voice behind her made Melanie freeze. She turned around slowly and found herself staring into Gina's wide and angry brown eyes.

Melanie felt the blood rush from her head to her feet and wondered how convenient it would be to faint right now. Oh, screw it. What good would that do? She'd already made a fool of herself with Taz. This was just icing on the cake. She straightened. Resigned but proud. "You heard me," she shot back, leveling a stare right back at that woman. "We aren't a couple. We barely know each other. The whole thing is a big fat lie, because you are such a—"

"Stop!"

The word burst from Taz. To say he was mad would be like saying the North Pole was cold or Mount Everest was tall. He was seething. His nostrils were flaring like a Spanish bull about to charge.

"Just stop," he repeated, more calmly. "You're making a scene."

She looked around. He was right. Everyone around them was looking in their direction. Her rage ebbed... until she saw Blond, Built, and Feathered trying to hide her face behind her hand, looking as if this were some unfortunate episode in her otherwise ultra-glamorous life. And looking at her with pity.

That changed everything.

Fresh rage filled Melanie. "Yeah, I'll stop," she snapped back with venom. "There's no need to get upset, right? That wasn't part of the bargain, was it? That wasn't part of our deal."

She turned and stormed into the crowd. She didn't have a direction, but somehow she ended up at the bar.

"A Sonic whatchamacallit," she said to the bartender when she caught her eye.

"Oh, my God, are you all right?"

It took a moment for Melanie to realize the comment was directed at her. She looked over her shoulder, and the alien cantina twins were standing behind her.

"I'm fine," she mumbled back, trying to sound like it were true.

"That must have been really awful for you," the chattier one said.

"It probably looked worse than it was," she replied. She paid the bartender, and took another gulp.

"If you say so," the young woman said. "Losing Taz Roman to his ex-girlfriend—"

Melanie picked up her drink. "Don't you get it? I didn't lose anything. We had a deal. He said he'd help me with my Divas audition, if I played nice. That's all it was."

The two women exchanged funny looks. The chattier one said, "So it was an arrangement? Like friends with benefits?"

"Yeah," Melanie said, but over their shoulders something caught her eye. "Yeah, something like that. I gotta go."

She took her drink and walked up to the tall, furry gladiator who was watching her from beneath a potted palm. Maybe she could salvage something of the night. Maybe she didn't have to go home alone and rejected after all.

She settled in beside him and said in her sexiest voice, "I hope this seat isn't taken."

"No way, sugar," he said. "It's been waiting for you all night."

CHAPTER THIRTY-THREE

MELANIE WAS STILL on the couch, beneath a pile of borrowed blankets, when Abby returned from her Sunday morning class at the dance studio.

"You can't sleep all day," she said, pulling back the vertical blinds and letting the sunshine spill into the living room.

Melanie scooted farther beneath the blankets.

"C'mon," Abby said, "I'll make you some pancakes, and you can tell me what happened. You can start by telling me why you were with a guy dressed as a dog in a gladiator costume. I thought you and Taz were going to the Pandemonium."

"We were. I mean, we did," Melanie grumbled, pushing herself to a sitting position. She instantly regretted it. Hangovers were a bitch.

"So what happened?" Abby said between the incredibly loud and painful clanking of pots and pans in the kitchen.

"His ex-girlfriend showed up, and Taz's sister found out we were faking the relationship."

"His ex blew your cover with his sister? That sucks." She walked out of the kitchen, holding a pancake box in each hand. "Blueberry or plain?"

"Plain," she said. "She didn't do it."

"What?"

"It's complicated," Melanie muttered. The whole horrid ordeal was coming back, despite her efforts to wash it away with alcohol. "Can we talk about something else?"

"Of course," her friend said. "But I'm curious. If his ex didn't blow your cover, how did his sister find out?"

"It was me, all right? I did it. He was acting like an ass, like I wasn't even there." Oh, God. She regretted the words the instant they were out.

Abby didn't say anything at first. But then she came out of the kitchen holding a plate full of pancakes soaked with syrup that she set on the coffee table, along with a fork and a knife. She dropped into the chair beside the couch. "So you were mad that he wasn't paying attention to you?"

"Yeah, sort of. I don't know. I guess."

"You know what that means, don't you?"

"Yeah," she said, digging into the food in front of her. "It means he's a class-A jerk."

Abby shook her head. "It means you fell for him."

"No, I didn't." Melanie speared a piece of pancake on her fork and then another. "He might not be as bad as I thought he was, but I didn't fall for him. I'm not that stupid."

Was she? Maybe for a minute, but not now.

"Okay, tell me what he did. Exactly."

"Why? So you can tell me what I already know?"

"Just humor me, all right?"

"Fine," she said and gave her friend the gritty details of the whole disaster.

When she finished, Abby stood and paced the living room, squeezing her lower lip in contemplation.

Melanie finished her pancakes.

Finally, Abby planted her hands on the back of the chair. "I hate to tell you this, but I think you're wrong. I think all that alcohol, your jealousy, or whatever it was messed with your head. All he did was talk to his ex. You're the one who left him alone with her. He never asked you to leave, did he?"

It *felt* like he wanted her to leave.

"Whose side are you on?"

"Yours! That's why I'm telling you you're crazy to give up over this. You obviously like him, and it seems to me—after everything you've said—that he probably has feelings for you too, because he had plenty of chances and plenty of reasons to tell you to get lost, and he didn't."

"Of course he did," Melanie protested. "I mean, he practically did. When he didn't—"

"When he didn't what? Blow off that woman fast enough for you? Refuse to speak to her, even though his sister probably dragged the poor woman halfway across the state? I'm sure he felt sorry for her. Seriously, Melanie, put yourself in his shoes."

Melanie opened her mouth to snap back another reply but clamped it shut instead. Her arguments weren't making sense anymore, not even to herself. No wonder her love life was always in shambles.

"So what am I supposed to do?"

Abby softened and smiled. "You could start by talking to him."

Melanie dropped her head in her hands and rubbed her eyes. "I suppose you're going to say I should apologize, too."

"I think you should start by just talking. The rest is up to you."

CHAPTER THIRTY-FOUR

THE STREETLIGHT IN front of Taz's house was out, making the cul-de-sac especially dark. Melanie pulled up along the curb. The gate was open, and she could see most of the windows were dark, except for one on the first floor. The Porsche was there, but the Escalade was gone. That was a relief. At least she wouldn't be running into Gina.

She ignored the voice inside telling her this was a mistake. The voice that kept her on the couch all day, drowning her hangover in gallons of water and pain relievers. Maybe Abby was right. Maybe she had gotten it all wrong last night. There was only one way to find out.

She focused on what she'd say: that she was sorry, that she shouldn't have stormed off. She'd tell him she'd been wrong and ask his forgiveness.

He could take it from there.

She walked up the pathway to the front door and spied him through the window, descending the stairs and turning toward the living room. He was gesturing, speaking to someone. Uh-oh. Gina was still there. That changed things.

That someone rounded the corner from the kitchen. Without her costume, it took a moment to recognize Tamara, looking fresh and clean. The gauzy pink dress she had on was even more flattering to her long, lean figure than that damn Big Bird Barbie costume.

Melanie stood still, her heart thudding like a jackhammer in her chest. She'd never be able to talk to him in front of Tamara. Hell, if that woman was here, there was no point in talking to him at all. She pinched her eyes shut. She should leave. She *wanted* to leave, but it was all she could do to stay on her feet. She closed her eyes and tried to get a grip on herself. If only every inch of her wasn't on the verge of crumpling to the ground. All she wanted to do was curl into a ball and shut everything out.

At first, the yipping sounded a million miles away. It took a few seconds to realize it was Spike on the other side of the door, barking her little canine head off. *Shit!* Melanie stumbled back and planted her foot in a hydrangea bush. "Damn it!" The words slipped out in a coarse whisper, but it was enough to send the dog into a heightened barking frenzy. Through the window, she saw Taz walking toward the door.

A spotlight hit her. Wait, no, not a spotlight. It was headlights. Melanie shielded her eyes and saw they were connected to the giant white Escalade pulling into the driveway.

Of course. Gina.

Melanie yanked her wedged-sandaled foot from the hydrangea tangle and stood with her hands up like a thief caught in a police sting.

"What are you doing here?"

Taz was standing in the open doorway, holding the still-yipping Spike in his arms. His voice was calm, but he didn't look happy to see her. Not in the slightest.

The dog squirmed out of his grasp, jumped to the ground, and raced to Melanie. She jumped to her kneecaps with loving excitement. It was impossible not to smile.

Before she could respond to Taz, Gina interjected: "You have a lot of nerve showing up here." She climbed down from the Escalade's passenger seat.

Taz leveled a hard stare at his sister. "Gina, that's enough."

"No, Tazarian, it's not enough. Not after what she did to you."

Tamara chose that moment to peek out from behind Taz, wrap her long arms around his shoulders and coo, "Oh, it's you."

That was all it took. Whatever hope Melanie had that she had misread Taz the night before was gone, vanished, *poof!*

"I just came for my stuff," she lied, "but obviously it was a mistake." She set down Spike, and the dog whimpered. It was comforting to know she hadn't misread *everybody*. She inched back toward the street. "If you could just drop my things off at the Shimmy Shop, that would be great."

She was about to add an apology, but the words stuck in her throat. Tears welled in her eyes. *Damn it!* She wasn't going to cry. She was *not* going to cry. She forced back the waterworks and forced her body not to betray her pain. She wasn't going to give any of them that satisfaction.

She spun around and hurried to the street. The pain seared through her like a hot knife, tearing apart every one of her hopes. By the time she reached her car, the tears dripped from her cheeks. She started the engine and pulled away. No one could see, none of them were even coming after her. In an instant, she knew she was utterly and completely alone.

CHAPTER THIRTY-FIVE

"WAS THAT THE girl?" Tamara asked in a saccharine tone.

"Yeah, that was Melanie," Taz replied. He removed the arm she had wrapped around his neck like a python.

Tamara scoffed. "She sure is a drama queen. You'd think she thought you were a real couple or something." She laughed her usual fake half-laugh, as if the idea were absurd. "You don't think she was getting the wrong idea, do you?"

Taz ignored her. Instead he bent down to scoop up Spike, who was whimpering and shivering at his ankle.

"I say good riddance," Gina added, clicking the key fob in her hand and making the Escalade chirp. "I can't believe she had the audacity to show her face around here. I think she knows now she isn't welcome."

"No kidding," Tamara chimed in. "Good riddance."

Taz clenched his teeth and closed his eyes. The pain at his temples was getting worse. He needed an aspirin or a shot of whiskey. Maybe both.

"At least it's over," his sister said. "You should count your blessings that it wasn't worse."

How in the world could it be worse? He didn't say the words. He rubbed between Spike's ears instead.

"I second that," Tamara said. "Anyone else hungry? I'm starving."

"You guys enjoy the pizza," he said and dug in his pocket for his keys.

"Where are you going?" Tamara asked.

He handed Spike to her, but the dog wiggled until Tamara set her inside the door. He watched Spike race back inside. That dog might be small, but she sure was smart.

He pulled his keys from his pocket. "I'm going for a drive."

"Can you at least get the box from the back seat?" Gina asked and blew on her nails. "I stopped for a manicure..."

That's how she'd turned what should have been a ten-minute pizza run into an hour-long event.

More games.

More bullshit.

He opened the Porsche's driver's side door and slid in behind the wheel. "I'm sure you'll manage. You always do."

"When will you be back?" Tamara whimpered.

He slammed the door. "I don't know," he said. He gunned the engine, and rolled onto the street without another look.

He had to get away. He had to think.

CHAPTER THIRTY-SIX

When Melanie pulled into the parking lot at Abby's apartment complex, she saw her friend walking to her car with an overnight bag slung over her shoulder.

Melanie flagged her down. "Where are you going?"

Abby hiked up the bag. "I'm staying at Derek's tonight. I figured it would be better than having him come here."

Melanie must have looked guilty, because Abby quickly added, "It's not a problem at all. I love having you here. And actually, he prefers it when I stay with him. He won't say it, but I know he misses the maid service when he's here. How did it go with Taz?"

"Don't ask."

"That bad, huh?" Abby looked away like she was sorry she'd asked.

"Hey, who cares, right? We had a fake relationship, so really it's just a fake break-up. No biggie." If only it *felt* like no biggie.

Abby opened the car door. "That's the right attitude. Hey, go ahead and help yourself to whatever's in the fridge. I also brought home a couple more old movies from the shop, if you're interested. Are you going to be all right on your own?"

Melanie ignored the gnawing feeling in her gut. The blackness pressing down on her. She scoffed. "Of course. Why wouldn't I be?"

She could tell Abby didn't believe it. She didn't blame her. She didn't really believe it, either.

"All right," Abby said warily. "Call me on my cell if you need anything."

"Go. Have fun." Melanie waved her off. "Tell Derek 'hi' for me."

"Okay, 'night," Abby said.

"'Night." Melanie waved and headed for the apartment.

Two seconds later, she heard Abby holler, "Hey, Melanie!"

She turned back.

Abby hadn't moved, and that worried look was still in her eyes. "I wasn't going to say anything, because it's just stupid gossip, but I think you should know, especially if Taz has already seen it. It sounds like he probably has."

Melanie frowned. "Seen what?"

"Like I said, it's stupid, and everyone will know it's a total lie, but you should probably check out the Scribbling Gypsy blog. There are some pictures from the Pandemonium Ball that you should see. Go ahead and use my computer."

All the terrible images came flooding back. The argument in the ballroom, the anger in Taz's eyes and the fury in Gina's. Those bloggers had been with her at the bar. They'd been friendly, even after the fight. "All right. I'll check it out."

"Call me if you want to talk about it."

"Okay," she said, but that only heightened her fear. How bad was it?

She let herself into the apartment with the spare key and bolted for the laptop Abby kept on her dinner table. She turned it on and drummed her fingers, waiting for the thing to boot up. It felt like an eternity before she could open the browser and type in the blog's address.

When the page came up, there were pictures from the party. Portraits of some of the costumes she'd seen. Many she hadn't. She scrolled down and found the one they'd taken of the Divas. All those happy, smiling faces. And then there was one of Taz, with Tamara, holding drinks and staring wide-eyed like a hunted animal caught in a trap.

A headline read, Taz the Romancer's Dirty Little Secret.

Her heart dropped.

Below it, she read: *We've always known Taz Roman is bad news, but it's even worse than we thought. A source tells us the local heartbreaker is now offering to pull strings at the upcoming auditions in return for certain favors—yes, those kinds of favors. Beware, ladies!*

Then it went on to other pictures, but Melanie couldn't see them. She couldn't see anything besides Taz's wide-eyed surprised expression.

This was all her fault. Her and her big, fat, stupid mouth.

No wonder he wouldn't speak to her. No wonder Gina wanted to rip her head off.

She needed to talk to him.

But trying that had already blown up in her face. Still, she grabbed her phone and scrolled. Huh? Oh, yeah. She'd only talked to him on Abby's studio phone.

Maybe she could email him?

She didn't have an email address, either.

She knew where he lived, that was it.

Should she go back?

No way. It took all of two seconds to realize what a terrible idea that was. She wasn't going to grovel in front of Tamara, especially when it was clear she and Taz were on the road to a reconciliation.

That thought ripped through her. It shouldn't hurt, she knew that. What happened last week was nothing more than friends with benefits. Hell, they were hardly even friends. She'd just let her stupid ideas run away with her.

Still, he deserved an apology, and he'd get it. She'd see him at the audition, and maybe by then his temper would be cooled.

But that didn't stop the adrenaline pumping through her veins or the whopping bruise on her pride. What she needed was about a gallon of chocolate ice cream and a bottle of red wine. Everything was better after ice cream and wine. If she remembered correctly, she'd seen a carton in Abby's fridge, and the girl always had a stash of decent reds in her pantry.

She went to the kitchen and pulled out the carton—vanilla with fudge swirl. Not ideal, but not bad. Behind the cheap reds at the front of the cabinet, she found a good Cabernet. French, from a region she couldn't even pronounce. Obviously, Abby was saving it for a special occasion, but this was an emergency. She made a mental note of the label so she could replace it, maybe before Abby even knew it was gone.

A few minutes later, she was changed into the yoga pants and T-shirt that passed as her pajamas, with a mixing bowl full of ice cream and a goblet full of red wine on the coffee table in front of the couch that was now her bed. She was about to grab the television remote control when she saw the DVDs. *Afrita Hanem* sat on the top. Her favorite Samia Gamal movie. Campy, sure—but also sweet. The dancing was fun and cheerful. Exactly what she needed tonight.

She pulled out the disc, fed it to the player, and sat back with her pity-party feast in front of her.

It didn't take long for the old black and white to work its charm. She lost herself in the story of the genie who loved her master so much, she didn't want to share him with anyone else. They were so perfect on screen, Samia and her leading man. It was easy to see their on-screen chemistry stemmed from feelings rooted in the real world.

There was obviously love between them, but there was also heartache. Probably more than anyone knew. Certainly more than Samia Gamal ever showed in her exuberant smiles and carefree dancing. It was a beautiful love story, Samia and Farid Al Atrache, but it must have been tragic, too, at least for Samia. Knowing her lover was pledged to another, and was unwilling to break those bonds to be with her.

But Samia never wavered. Not like Melanie was doing. Where did she find the strength? How could she hide her pain? As Melanie watched her movie-star idol flit across the screen in another joyous dance, it became clear. Samia was a dancer. Whatever pain, whatever heartache she felt, she must have absorbed it into her dance. No matter what Farid did, no matter what any man did, she could always dance.

That was what Melanie was going to do, too.

CHAPTER THIRTY-SEVEN

THE NEXT DAY, Melanie felt better—she had a purpose again. But attitude was only going to get her so far. In the cool gray morning, before work, she took a detour to the Bella Garden mobile home park. She told herself she needed to grab work clothes and practice gear, since hers was being held hostage at Taz's house.

Even as she told herself that, she knew there was another reason, too. In spite of all her faults and all the turmoil between them, Ginger was still her mother, and right now she wanted her mom.

She eased up to the trailer and caught the glowing flicker of the television through the window. A moment later, she knocked on the front door.

"I don't want any," Ginger bellowed from inside. "Take your magazines or your candy bars or whatever, and keep moving."

Melanie rested her forehead on the door. "Mom, it's me." When she didn't hear anything, she turned the knob. It was unlocked, and she pushed it open gently.

"You busy?" she asked, peeking her head in. "I need to pick up a few things."

"Fine," Ginger said, shifting in her recliner, empty soda cans littering the floor around her, her bad foot propped on the foot rest. "Do what you want. You always do."

Melanie left the barb alone. She wasn't here to argue. She made her way back to the spare bedroom, where her boxes were and pulled out a few blouses, a pair of jeans, and leggings. Hell, she threw it all back in the box and hoisted it. She might as well take the whole thing. She muscled it to the dinette table, where she set it down with a thump. She went to the refrigerator. "Mind if I get a drink?"

"I guess that means you're sticking around a while. That's a change."

"I didn't come to fight with you, Ma," she said in her most even, most non-confrontational tone. She grabbed a can of diet cola and dropped into one of the dinette chairs. "I just need to pick up some things for work and the audition."

Her mother never took her eyes off the television. "So you're going through with that nonsense, then?"

"Yes, I'm going through with it."

"Suit yourself. If you want to make the biggest mistake of your life, who am I to stop you?"

"It isn't a mistake."

Ginger Drake smirked and kept her eyes on her television.

Melanie stiffened. "I'm a good dancer, Ma. I'm better than good."

"If you say so."

"I do say so."

Ginger stabbed at the remote control and muted the sound. "I just don't want you to get your hopes up. You know what happens when girls like you get their hopes up. You get hurt, and the world doesn't care. Look at me. I can sit here and rot in this trailer and who's going to care? No one."

The words cut but only for an instant. In that moment, she realized her mother wasn't talking about her. Maybe she'd stopped talking about her years ago, and Melanie had just stopped listening. "It doesn't have to be that way for you. No one forces you to stay in here. You can leave any time."

Ginger scoffed. "You know that's not true. What about my foot?"

"That's an excuse. I've seen you walk all over this trailer just fine. I've seen you spring to the window when you hear the man next door watering his flower box. Why don't you just fix yourself up, and go over there? Talk to him. Talk to someone."

Her mother shifted and seemed to sink deeper in the recliner. "You know why I can't. I have bunions. They hurt too bad."

"I know they don't hurt nearly as bad as you pretend they do." She was getting bolder. She'd never spoken to her mother this way. "Whatever is keeping you here, you need to get over it. You got laid off. You don't have to lie about it. It happens. You don't have to be embarrassed."

"Why would you say that? Were you sneaking through my things?"

"I didn't go through your things. It was a guess, but one I should have made weeks ago. I should have known you of all people wouldn't let something like bunions keep you off your feet. You, who goes to the doctor for cough syrup, refusing to go for this? It means you lost your insurance because you lost your job. I didn't know for sure till I called the supermarket and asked."

"You had no right to do that. That's an invasion of my privacy."

"You're right. I probably shouldn't have done it. I wouldn't have had to if there weren't so many lies between us."

Ginger folded her arms into a brick wall that separated them.

Melanie knew she should stop. They'd said more today than they'd said in months. Years, maybe. The wound was already open. She might as well say everything. "Since we're on the topic of the truth," she began, "I want to know why my father left, and I want the truth."

Ginger scoffed, but her arms pulled more tightly across her chest. "I've told you why a hundred times. He didn't want a family. He said he didn't need that kind of headache in his life. He was a coward."

Melanie took a deep breath. It was now or never. "Really, Ma? I'm not sure I believe that anymore. I think it was you."

"How dare you! That's not true."

"Isn't it? The more I think about that time, the more I remember. I remember that he tried to come back, and you wouldn't let him."

"That's a lie."

Melanie left the chair and kneeled by her mother so she could look her in the eye. She wanted her to see she wasn't being nasty. She just wanted to finally know the truth.

"I believe you think it's a lie." She put her hand on her mother's forearm and felt the muscles twitch in defense. "I believe you think it because if you didn't, you'd have to realize that I'm not the reason you're miserable. I'm not the reason your life was ruined. It's not my fault, Mama." Melanie's voice cracked with the emotion she'd ignored for years.

She had been thinking about these words, repeating them in her brain until they formed ruts. The words didn't come out as smoothly as she had imagined. They snagged and sliced through her, fighting her every inch of the way. It was not easy saying these things to her mother. She had accepted the woman's hatred for so long.

She'd accept it still, but she had to know the truth.

The air crackled with tense silence, filled only with the muted voices on the television. Her words had sucked the air from the room. Not just the air, it took away the tension. The worry. It was almost peaceful.

A ray of sunshine peeked through a slit in the curtains. Melanie went to them and pulled them open, letting light spill into rooms that had not seen it in far too long. The brightness played off the dust that danced in the air. The cobwebs that filled the gap between the curtain and the glass. The dead flies lying on the sill.

Her mother winced and glanced away.

"Don't open that. You know it gives me headaches."

"It's only because you hide away in here. And you know, you're right about one thing. It has been partly my fault, because I've let you do this. But I won't anymore. I won't let you wallow away your life. You've made yourself miserable, and you can't do that anymore. You have to get out into the world and see what you're missing."

"There's just a bunch of crap and criminals out there," Ginger grumbled.

"Sure, but there's also a whole wonderful world. There's blue sky and cool breezes. When was the last time you saw the sun set over Catalina Island? When was the last time you walked along the shore? Those things you talk about are still out there. You can still enjoy them. You still have a life, even if you don't want to admit it."

"I don't need a lecture from my daughter. My daughter, who doesn't even have a place to live and can't keep a boyfriend."

Melanie felt her chest swell with rage. That's what her mother wanted. She wanted a fight. Fighting was all she knew. If they were going to break the cycle, Melanie had to be the one to stop it. She had to make the change.

"I'm fine, Ma. You don't have to worry about me."

"But you're alone," her mother said. "Aren't you afraid you'll end up alone for the rest of your life, like…" Her voice trailed off, but Melanie knew what she couldn't say.

"No, Ma. I'm not afraid of that anymore."

CHAPTER THIRTY-EIGHT

BY THE TIME Melanie walked into work, Deffner was already in his office. She slipped into her chair, started up her computer, and tried to look busy. If she were lucky, he might not notice she was nearly an hour late.

She wasn't lucky.

"About time you showed up," he said before she'd even tucked her purse in her bottom desk drawer. He dropped a stack of invoices on her desk. "I need you to log these into the system before lunch so they can get into this month's expenses run. I also want you to sit down with the new file clerk. She's filing last year's reports in this year's files. The auditors are going ballistic."

"Can't the file supervisor do it?" She was the girl's boss, after all.

"You know Josephine. She's already got one clerk out for stress or fatigue or whatever bullshit and another one who's complaining to Human Resources every other day. She's terrible at these kinds of things. Can you just handle it?"

"Fine, I'll do it."

There was no use arguing that a manager should have to do the manager's job or that it would take superhuman data-entry skills to get a stack like that logged before lunch. Deffner didn't care about facts. He just wanted results, and for better or worse he relied on Melanie for those results. In the beginning, she liked the extra responsibility. She liked that he relied on her. Now, it was just more shit to shovel.

It wasn't that Deffner wasn't grateful. He was always grateful. While he couldn't make up for the extra work with a bigger salary—she had reached the top of her pay grade ages ago—he tried to make up for it with the lenient four-ten work week and not docking her when she'd slide into work an hour late.

Lately, though, it just wasn't enough. Every day since she'd made the decision to audition, to actually go for her dream, her time on the fourth floor of the *Orange County Herald* seemed like a waste of time. Even now, with that stack of invoices staring her in the face, she couldn't muster the effort to get them logged into the system.

She glanced at the calendar, and there it was, circled in fat, red marker: the day of the audition. Just five measly days separated her from that moment and—with any luck—her destiny.

But she couldn't rely on luck. Not this time. She'd worked too hard for it, sacrificed too much. Not to mention making a fool of herself with Taz Roman.

She was not going to be like her mother. She wasn't going to sit around and complain about the raw deal she'd been dealt in life. She was going to make this happen. She *had* to make this happen.

She stared at the invoices. She stared at the calendar. She closed her eyes and took a deep breath. She knew what to do.

CHAPTER THIRTY-NINE

"WOW, THE PLACE looks great," Melanie said, taking in the improvements at the Shimmy Shop boutique.

Abby was on her knees, wiping the front of the glass case filled with beaded costumes imported from Egypt. She finished and stood with a proud grin. "It really does, doesn't it? I can't believe it's real. You know, I couldn't have done it without you."

Melanie laughed. "Sure, if unpacking a few boxes counts. Give credit where it's due: you made this happen all by yourself."

Abby checked the clock. "So what's up? Ten o'clock is kind of early for a lunch break."

"I'm not on lunch. I'm on vacation."

"How'd Deffner take that?"

"About as well as you'd expect, but I'm worthless there anyway. I can't think about anything but the audition. I told him I needed to take a few days. He wasn't happy, but there was really nothing he could do about it. If I don't use my two weeks by the end of the summer, I'll lose them. I'm not going to let that happen."

"Good for you," Abby said. "And honestly I'm not surprised. I know how hard you're working for this audition. I'm proud of you."

"Thanks. I'm proud of you, too. You've made this place amazing. When is the grand opening?"

Abby's smile vanished. "As soon as I find a manager."

"I thought you were going to ask Janaya."

"I did. She's not interested. Said she doesn't have the time."

"Really? What's she doing besides teaching classes here?"

"You mean besides dating every guy who crosses her path? I honestly don't know. You should hear her stories, though. After-hour parties, private clubs, spur-of-the-moment trips. That girl has a social calendar that would put a Kardashian to shame."

"How's she afford all that?"

"Beats me. It never seems to be an issue."

"Must be nice."

"No kidding. If you know anybody who's looking for a job, send them my way."

"I'm happy to help."

Abby waved her off. "I know, but that would only be a temporary solution. Once you ace the audition, you'll be gone."

"I appreciate your confidence, but it's not exactly a sure thing."

"It might as well be. Speaking of that, have you talked to Taz yet?"

Melanie's gaze dropped to the floor. She shook her head. Between everything with her mom and her job, she'd talked herself into putting that awkward conversation off. "I decided I'm going to get to the audition early and talk to him then."

"Are you sure you want to wait that long?"

"I don't have another way of getting in touch with him without going back to his place, and I'm not going back there."

"I'm sure I have a phone number for him, or an email address."

Yeah, she was afraid of that. "Thanks," she said in her best backtracking voice. "But honestly, if I ask him to meet me, I doubt he would. Things were really bad the last time I saw him."

Abby got quiet then said, "I saw him this morning. He came by a couple hours ago to drop off more CDs. He left something for you."

Melanie's heart sank. She knew it couldn't be good if her friend had taken this long to tell her. When Abby returned with her familiar duffel bag, it sank again. Of course it was just the stuff she'd left at his place.

She took it from Abby. "Did he say anything? I mean, about me?"

Abby looked away. "No. He was in a hurry. He only stopped in for a minute."

It didn't surprise her, but the news stung just the same. "I guess I should be glad he didn't burn my stuff, or let Gina do it. I'm sure she would have liked to."

Abby made a face. "I don't know. Taz doesn't seem like the vindictive type, but I suppose you know him better than I do."

Melanie was quiet. She thought she had known him, but did she really? The Taz she thought she knew wouldn't have welcomed back the woman who had broken his heart. But he had, hadn't he? It just proved what she didn't want to admit to herself: that she'd never known him at all. And worse, he'd never had feelings for her.

"Is it all right if I use the dance room for a little bit? I thought I'd get some practice in."

"Yeah, sure," Abby said. "It'll be empty all day. Janaya had to cancel tonight's class, and I don't have the energy to cover it."

Melanie rallied. "You should have said something. I can do it."

"You don't have to. I know you're busy."

"I'm not too busy to help a friend," she said. "Come on, let me do it."

Abby scratched at the edge of her mouth and looked like she was mulling something over. Melanie knew that look enough to fear it.

"Okay, spill it."

"There's nothing to spill. I was just wondering."

Abby was trying far too hard to look casual. There was something brewing beneath that long, black ponytail. Something devious.

"Fine. I'll bite. What are you wondering?"

"Derek and I were talking last night, and he mentioned that he has this friend—"

Melanie hid her face in her hands. "Oh, God. Now I'm the poor friend who needs everybody's pity."

"No, that's not what I'm saying."

"Really? Because that's what I'm hearing."

"Why don't you let me finish before you start complaining?"

"You're right. Please, continue."

"Derek and I were talking. He mentioned that a friend from the Montana newspaper where he worked is in town. He'd like to introduce him to some of the nightlife. Nobody likes to be a third wheel, so he wondered if I knew anyone who might join us."

"So it's a blind date? You know I hate blind dates."

"It's not. It's just dinner with a few friends. No expectations. Just dinner."

"Just dinner?"

"Maybe drinks afterward, but that's it."

"So dinner and drinks. Where?"

Abby perked up. "You're going to like this: we're taking him to Delaney's."

"Delaney's on the Pier? The crazy-expensive Delaney's on the Pier?"

"Mmm-hmm, and drinks at the Blue Thistle afterward."

"Who's playing?"

"Does it matter? If they're playing the Thistle, they've got to be good."

It was true. The Thistle was one of the best local venues for live music, and it didn't hurt that it was steps from the Newport Beach surf.

"Okay, let me think about it."

Abby smiled like she had a secret weapon.

"What?"

"Well, I should probably also mention that he's totally hot. I'm taking Derek's word for it, of course, but he said Cole had women lining up at the paper where they worked."

Melanie laughed. "You had me at free dinner at Delaney's, which is a good thing, because I'm certainly not taking your boyfriend's word for it when it comes to rating guys. Sorry."

"Suit yourself." Abby shrugged, but she still looked pleased with herself.

CHAPTER FORTY

THE MUSIC ROOM'S door flew open, barely missing the drum Taz had set down while he scribbled notes on the tattered, handwritten sheet music on his stand.

"Hey, ever hear of knocking?" he snapped at Gina.

She walked across the room and plucked the bulky headphones off his head.

"You don't have to yell," she complained. "I did knock. I've been knocking all day, but you've been hiding beneath these things." She shook the headphones at him to emphasize her point.

He stared at his music, wishing she would just go back to New York. Hell, she could go anywhere, as long as it was far away. "I'm not hiding. I'm working."

"Really? That's interesting, because Garrett just called. He wants to know when you're coming in to the office. He said you've blown off two meetings about the tour."

The anger simmering in his gut erupted to a full boil. "Why are you answering my phone? You just can't keep your nose out of my business, can you?"

"What's gotten into you? I'm here, trying to help and all—"

"Help? Is that what you call it?" He tried to laugh, but it came out like scoff. He ran his fingers through his hair and clenched his eyes shut. *I don't need this, not now.*

"I didn't tell him anything. I didn't even tell him you were home, but you can't just lock yourself up in this room. You're going to have to talk to him eventually. Wouldn't it be better if he heard your side first? Before someone else tells him?"

He looked at her and shook his head. For someone who considered herself so much smarter than everyone else, she could be incredibly dumb.

"He already knows," he said with forced calm. "I'm sure he's known since the damn thing hit the Internet."

"You don't know that. Don't assume—"

"I know," he said with a finality that shut her up. "What I don't know is why you care. This is what you wanted, isn't it? It got rid of Melanie."

He had more to say, but mentioning her name unexpectedly stopped him short. He could still see the way she looked the night she came back. The shame, the uncertainty. She said she'd come back for her things, but was that it? If only Tamara had stayed inside.

No, you idiot. It wouldn't have mattered. It never mattered. It was all fake. Every minute of it.

He swallowed the lump rising in his throat.

Gina pounced. "How can you say that's what I wanted? I'm just looking out for you."

Of course she was going to put on the innocent act now that the damage was done.

"Why else would you lure Tamara here? You had your mind made up the minute you met Melanie, maybe even before."

His sister straightened. "I never wanted to hurt you. I just thought there might be unfinished business between you and Tamara. That's certainly the impression she gave me."

"She gave you? Great. I'm so glad the two of you have gotten so close."

"You know she feels terrible about what happened. People make mistakes. Can you blame her for wanting to make amends? You really didn't have to chase her off to some hotel like she was a common—"

He jumped up and nearly knocked over the music stand. "You had no right to tell her she could stay here. You don't live here anymore. Don't you understand that? You can't control everything. You can't control *me*."

She folded her arms in that motherly pose that made his skin crawl.

"I'm not trying to control you. I'm sorry you felt the need to put on a big charade to avoid my uncomfortable questions. This is not what I wanted," she said. "Certainly not like this."

He slanted a curious look at her. "Not like what?"

"Well, you know, the way it looks," she sputtered.

"No, tell me. How does it look?"

"You know," she said, her eyes darting around the room but finding nowhere safe to land. "There's Mom and Dad's legacy to think about. It doesn't honor their memory to have our name dredged through the mud like this."

His palm flew to his forehead. Now it was making sense.

"Our name," he repeated. "Not *my* name but the *family* name. That's why you're concerned?"

Her face twisted. "Well, yeah. What do you think they would say about all this?"

"I've been thinking about that a lot these past few days. In a way, I think that's all I've been thinking about. I didn't have an answer before, but I think I do now. Mom and Dad would say, 'Live your life.' You have your life. You have a husband and a new home. I don't know if you're happy or not, but you have your own life. Now, I think it's time I stop following the path everyone else thinks I should follow, and find my own."

She shook her head. "Wait, what's that mean?"

He smiled, and for the first time in days, it was genuine. He threw up his hands and shrugged. "I don't know exactly, but I'm going to find out. First, I'm going to go see Garrett." He brushed past her as he headed for the door. He stopped and turned back.

"I think you should be gone by the time I get back. I'm not angry, but I'm finished with letting you meddle in my life." He walked back, took her by both shoulders, and kissed the top of her head. "I love you, but you need to leave."

CHAPTER FORTY-ONE

TURNED OUT, DEREK was right on the money. Cole Winston was indeed hot.

Sure, there was the crease his cowboy hat left in his hair, bleached blond by the sun and trimmed short above the ears, and the western shirt that apparently passed as evening attire where he was from. But when his rosy lips pulled into a smile and his baby blues sparkled at the sight of her walking in with Abby, it made her knees turn to jelly.

"I told you he was handsome," Abby whispered as they sashayed through Delaney's bustling bar to join the guys at a cocktail table by the window. "Please be nice to him."

"I'll be nice," she said.

Derek and Cole stood when they approached, and Cole tapped Derek's chest good-naturedly. "You didn't tell me we were going to have company. Such lovely company as this, no less."

"I thought you might enjoy looking at somebody besides me today," Derek said, obviously pleased at Cole's reaction.

After the introductions were made, Cole took Abby's hand and shook it, then Melanie's hand, which he lifted slowly to his lips and kissed. "The pleasure is all mine," he said.

Ordinarily, a hokey line like that would make her groan. From him it sounded unexpectedly sweet and sincere. She stifled the smile growing within her.

"Derek has been extolling the virtues of living in this Orange County of yours," Cole said. "I'll be honest and say I am not a big fan of the freeways or the hurry everyone seems to be in, but"—he turned to the window—"this view of the ocean"—he turned back and planted his gaze squarely on Melanie—"and the view in here is beginning to grow on me."

"I told him," Derek said, "with his head for numbers, he can pretty much write his own ticket in this town. Of course, I'm selfish and hoping he'll take my offer to join the *Herald*."

Cole smiled sheepishly, but he was saved from having to reply by the arrival of the hostess.

"Your table's ready," she said and led them to a cozy booth in a dimly lit corner of the restaurant.

For the next hour and a half, Cole guided the conversation away from work and skillfully coaxed information out of Abby and Melanie without seeming nosy. He was easy to like and doing everything but wave a sign that said he was interested in her. It would have made for a perfect night if she could stop comparing everything about him to Taz. Shorter hair, taller, and leaner build. A softer, quieter way about him, a way that deflected rather than grabbed the spotlight. He was such a gentleman, he didn't even snap back when she tossed a snarky comment his way. Not the way Taz did. But that was better, right?

She told herself it was.

"So what kind of music do you listen to, Cole?" The abruptness of her question surprised even her. She reached over and took another sip of her red wine and smiled like it was just a casual question.

He glanced down at his western shirt, and chuckled. "Here I thought the cowboy shirt and boots would give me away. I'm flattered that you don't assume I'm a good ol' country boy. The truth is, I like all sorts of music. Haven't kept up with the new music much, but I'm a fan of the classics. You know, Zeppelin, Van Halen, Rem."

"You mean R.E.M.?" she said with more attitude than she'd intended.

He blushed. "Yeah, R.E.M. Like I said, music isn't really my thing."

She didn't have to look at Abby to know her friend was giving her the "knock it off" look. She knew she was being a jerk, and she knew Cole didn't deserve it. She just couldn't stop herself. The more she looked at him and the more he spoke, the more she ached for Taz.

She pushed her chair back, removed the napkin from her lap, and grabbed her purse. "I'll be back in a minute," she said and bolted for the ladies' room.

She was in the stall with the door closed when Abby walked in after her, but she knew it was her even before she said, "Melanie, are you in here?"

"Yeah," she said. "You don't have to say anything. I know I was awful. I don't know why... no, that's not true. I know, but it's no excuse."

"What happened? Cole is a great guy. I thought you were hitting it off."

"You're right, he's great. He's awesome."

"But?"

Melanie stood up, still fully dressed, and walked out of the stall to face her friend. "I don't know. He's just so country, and he doesn't know about music. How can I be with someone who doesn't know anything about music?"

"Basically it's because he's not Taz?"

Melanie sneered. "No, that's not it. It has nothing to do with Taz."

Did it?

"I'm not pining for Taz. I don't pine after anybody. I never do. I never have. That's why it's so stupid to fall in love, because you just end up feeling like shit."

Abby sucked in her lips. She had something to say, but she wasn't saying it.

"What?" Melanie demanded, growing angrier by the second. "Why are you smirking at me?"

"I'm sorry. I'm not smirking. I never said you were pining for Taz. You said it. Actually, you said it twice, and you also mentioned love."

"No, I didn't."

Abby made a face.

"If I did, I was just making a point."

"To me? Or to yourself?"

It really sucked when Abby got like this, so patronizing and smug. It was completely infuriating, because now it was obvious. And she didn't like it.

"I'm going to go insane if I stay here another minute."

CHAPTER FORTY-TWO

MELANIE LET HERSELF in and switched on the lights. The studio looked so different at night. So silent and still. She could hear the traffic on busy Newport Boulevard, and the deep growl of a Harley cruising toward the beach.

It was only eight thirty, but most of the shops in the corner shopping center were already closed. Only the liquor store at the end was open, and it appeared to be doing a brisk business.

She turned the lock behind her, leaned against the cool plate glass, and took a deep breath.

When she told Abby she had to leave, she hadn't intended to come to the studio. She hadn't thought that far ahead, but it was perfect. She reminded herself mentally to thank Abby for shoving the keys in her hand and telling her to go.

She took another deep, restorative breath then looked down at her miniskirt and strappy sandals. The skirt was great for showing off her cherry blossom tattoo, but it wouldn't make it through a minute of her dance routine. She eyed the newly arranged clothes racks in the boutique.

Abby wouldn't mind a couple early sales.

She flipped through the stretchy yoga pants and settled on a black pair with "Belly Dancer" screened in red in a flattering arch over the rear. She grabbed a matching red mini-tank and stopped by the cash register to leave a note for Abby.

While she scribbled her IOU, she noticed a CD jewel case with a sticky note attached. She picked it up, and her chest tightened. In barely legible chicken scratch, it read, "A few experimental tracks. Tell me what you think, Taz." Below his name was a phone number and an email address.

He must have dropped it off when he dropped off her stuff. Why hadn't Abby mentioned it? But her frustration with Abby took a back seat to her curiosity.

What was on this disc? Were these new tracks for his solo album?

Only one way to find out.

She marched to the dance room and fed the disc to the stereo. A moment later, the speakers filled the room with a lively drum solo, but it wasn't like any solo she'd ever heard before. It was Middle Eastern, but there were also Latin rhythms and—what was that? Greek? Romani? It was like a United Nations of sounds, blending a world of influences into a single, amazing piece of music that made her hips shake and her shoulders shimmy.

Without realizing it, she was moving around the dance floor, translating the tempo into rapid-fire hip drops and the slower transitions into floating arms and hand flourishes. This music was infectious, and in an instant she knew this was the music of his heart. This was the kind of music his father had played. That was what he wanted to bring back to preserve his father's legacy.

There was not just one track. She discovered there were four, all different, but all a wonderful musical bridge of world beats, yet there was something very Taz in the music, too. In her mind, she could see him playing this music in his recording room, striking every note, every chord.

Even more, she could feel how much the music meant to him. His intensity, his passion was as much a part of that recording as the music. She could feel him giving everything to that moment, just as he had given to her that night they'd spent together. She could feel the strength in his hands, not on the drum skin, but on her own skin, his fingertips traveling along every contour of her body, and directing all of that intensity onto her.

Had she really been so wrong about him? The music told her she wasn't, and his music didn't lie. He put his heart and soul into it. So why was it so hard to believe he could put just as much of himself into his feelings for her?

Why had she run at the first opportunity?

Now that was clear, too. Just like Abby had said, he hadn't done anything besides talk to Tamara. Melanie had done the rest.

The truth was, she owed him much more than an apology, and it couldn't wait five more days. It couldn't wait one more day.

She didn't even have to go back to the counter to retrieve his phone number, because the image of it was branded on her brain.

She fished her cell phone out of her purse and dialed.

CHAPTER FORTY-THREE

TAZ DIDN'T RETURN the call that night or the next day. He didn't return the call at all. Melanie wanted to call again, but she couldn't muster the courage. If he wanted to talk, he'd call. She had to accept that he wasn't interested. Plain and simple.

The message he was sending was clear enough: back off.

So she did. Every time he worked his way into her thoughts, she focused harder on the audition. *This* was what was important, she reminded herself. This was what mattered.

She danced until she was exhausted, and then she danced more. She danced till every limb felt like pudding.

When she was finally too tired to dance, she went through her wardrobe, trying to decide what to wear, how to wear her makeup, or style her hair. She settled on something one day, second-guessed it the next, and started again at least a dozen times.

The morning of the audition, she had narrowed the search to either a teal tiered skirt, plum harem pants, and a matching choli, or a pair of black flared-leg pants with lettuce edges and an imported cherry silk choli.

She was trying on the flared-leg pants one more time when she heard a rip and saw bare skin where the rear seam should be.

"Great," she mumbled. She slipped them off and tossed them over a chair. "Better here than in front of a roomful of judges, I guess."

Ten minutes later she was dressed in the teal and plum outfit, with her music, dance shoes, and other essentials packed in her duffel bag. On her way out, Abby thrust a travel mug of fresh coffee in her hand.

"Are you sure you don't want me to come along for moral support?" Abby asked for probably the tenth time in two days.

"No, you'll only make me more nervous." She sipped the coffee—oh, it was heaven—and made her way to the door.

She wasn't going to mention that it was the prospect of seeing Taz again that had her stomach in knots. She'd gone over in her mind exactly what she wanted to say and how she would say it. She knew he was going to be angry, but she also knew it didn't matter. She had to do this. He had to know she never meant to hurt him.

In her car, she was still so focused on rehearsing her speech that she stepped on the gas instead of the brake when she put the car into gear. The vehicle lurched violently, and the engine died.

She stared at the hot, brown liquid pooling in her lap. The coffee mug was no longer standing securely in the cup holder in the center console, but had jumped out of that pocket and was lying on its side, dribbling its contents onto her skirt and turning the beautiful teal into a dingy and wet brown mess.

She wanted to crumple into a ball of tears, but there wasn't time. She had given herself twenty minutes to get to the theater, which should have been plenty of time to park and find where she was supposed to check in before the eleven o'clock call time.

She returned the now-empty cup to the cup holder, jumped out of the car, pulled a spare towel from the back, and pushed it into the worst of the spill. Then she made her way back to the apartment.

When she rushed in, Abby was on the couch with the newspaper. "Did you forget some—oh, no."

"Yeah, coffee catastrophe. I don't have time for this." By the time she finished her sentence, she was already in the bathroom and shimmying out of the wet skirt. She soaked up the excess liquid with a towel and then ran it under the running faucet until the stain diminished.

"Let me do that one," Abby said, edging her away from the sink. "You take care of the harem pants in the kitchen."

Melanie looked down. The harem pants were in bad shape too. She did as Abby said, yanked off the harem pants, and made her way in her panties to the kitchen. She was already running water over them when she realized the balcony blinds were open and the older couple who lived across the path were sitting on their patio. The man had obviously seen something, because he was being less than subtle about craning his head to get a better view of her now that there was a breakfast counter between him and her underwear.

Melanie pulled a dish towel from the counter and did her best to cover up her lacy, black underthings as she made her way back to the window to draw the blinds. The man was still craning, but his wife must have figured out what was up, because she was swatting his shoulder. He had the gall to act indignant. "Whatever, you pervert," Melanie said under her breath and hurried back to the faucet.

"I think I got it all out of the skirt," Abby hollered. "How are you doing?"

"It's coming out, but they're soaked." She bit back the curse she wanted to hurl at them, at anyone who would listen.

"You must have something else to wear."

Melanie tensed her face, squishing her eyelids, her lips, her nose. "I did until I split a seam in the pants. I'd rather not be 'that girl with the torn pants,' but it looks like that's what it's going to be. Do you have any safety pins I could borrow?"

"Hold on, I have an idea."

A moment later, Melanie heard the whine of a hair dryer. "The fabric is so thin, I think this'll work. Bring yours."

By the time Melanie brought in the wad of wet harem pants that she'd wrapped tightly in a towel, Abby had nearly a yard of the ten-yard skirt dry. "Here, use your dryer." She handed Melanie her travel-size model.

Melanie grabbed an extra hanger, fastened the waistband to its clips, and hung the harem pants from the towel rack as Abby had done. She got to work.

Before long, both garments were mostly dry.

"That's good enough," Melanie said. She pulled them back on, grabbed and hugged Abby, and hurried out the door, slowing just long enough to catch the time on the microwave on her way out. Eleven twenty.

She groaned, but she didn't stop.

She jumped back in her car and didn't stop, didn't let herself think, until she was standing in front of the silent theater, staring at the sign taped to the door.

"Belly Dance Divas Inside" was scrawled in black marker. This was it. All the talk, all the preparation, everything came down to this. Whatever happened on the other side of this glass was going to change everything.

"Here for the audition?"

Melanie wheeled around to find a stout woman with fluffy, burgundy hair shuffling toward her. She held a clipboard with a pen dangling from a string that bobbed nearly to her Birkenstocks.

Melanie hiked her dance bag higher on her shoulder and tried to ignore the still-damp feeling of the fabric against her thighs. "Yeah. Am I in the right place?"

"You're late."

"I know, I'm sorry, it was—"

The woman waved her hand in a gesture that said, "I don't care."

"Are you registered?"

"Yeah, I submitted the application online a few days ago."

The woman nodded. "Name?"

Melanie told her.

The woman flipped pages on her clipboard, stopped at one, and scanned it with her fingertip. She paused. One eyebrow lifted. She glanced up. "You're a friend of Taz Roman?"

What kind of question was that? "Sort of," she answered.

"Interesting."

Before Melanie could ask why, the woman pulled open the door and pointed to a wall of doors across the lobby.

"Follow the duct-tape arrows on the floor to the check-in room. Let them know you're here, and they'll give you a number and show you where to wait."

Melanie crossed the floor and wondered what was on that sheet to indicate she knew Taz. Had he left a note? Was she already doomed?

She didn't have time to worry about that, though, because when she opened the door to the check-in room, she got her first look at the competition. She'd expected dozens, but there had to be more than a hundred women in there. Tribal dancers, cabaret dancers, fusion dancers—even goth dancers.

A young man with platinum, spiked hair and a lanyard around his neck sat behind a folding table. In front of him was a line at least twenty dancers deep. She stepped behind the last one.

A half hour later, when she reached the front, she gave him her name and he found her on his check-in sheet.

She watched his expression. There it was. A slight downturn of his lips. Was it surprise or disapproval? She couldn't tell.

"Why do people keep doing that?"

He looked up. "Doing what?"

"Why do you all look so surprised when you see my name on the sheet? What's it say there?"

He leaned forward and rested his arms on the sheet, covering what little she could see. "I don't know what you mean, but if you'll just pin this to your shirt." He slid over a laminated card with the number 124.

She glanced back. There was no one behind her and no one within earshot. As she leaned forward to pick it up, she asked, "Is Taz Roman around?"

The guy's expression contorted. "I doubt it. You know he's not going to be with the tour this year, right?"

It was like the ground gave out beneath her.

"Why not?"

The guy shrugged. "I couldn't say," he said, though he looked like he knew more. "If you'll have a seat, we'll call your number when it's your turn. I suggest you get comfortable. It's going to be awhile."

She grabbed her dance bag and turned toward the mass of folding chairs and bodies in various stages of warm-up, chill-out, and deep concentration. Finally, she was here. She was in. No more drama or obstacles.

She should have felt excited or at least relieved. So why did she feel so miserable?

CHAPTER FORTY-FOUR

MELANIE RUSHED TO the bathroom, overcome by nausea. It all made sense now. Everything Gina had said, the reason Taz hadn't called her back. The bloggers were right. This was all her fault. Melanie had done this, with that one stupid and spiteful remark.

How could she have believed he would quit? Of course he wouldn't. He loved the show. He lived for it. And she'd gotten him fired.

The sick feeling subsided. She wrapped her arms around her middle and tried to make sense of what she'd heard. She was stunned by what it all meant.

She swiped at a runaway tear, and her arm brushed the number pinned to her chest. She pressed it to her skin. The reminder why she was here. The reminder it was all she had left.

She had to pull herself together. No matter what it took, she had to make it through the next couple hours.

It took every ounce of determination she possessed not to run out of the building, but finally she was standing in the wings, watching number 123 perform on the stage. The dancer was pure Egyptian cabaret with a strong ballet flair. Pointe shoes, pirouettes, the whole shebang. It looked great.

Melanie found herself enjoying the show before she remembered this was a competition. The woman wasn't that great, Melanie told herself. And what had Taz told her? Garrett preferred more belly than ballet in his dancers. It gave her hope.

The dancer's music was beginning to wind down when a shout came from the audience seats.

"Thank you," the voice hollered abruptly. "We'll be in touch."

All the stage makeup, all that glitter and poise, none of it hid the woman's disappointment. She moved quickly offstage, and Melanie could feel the heartbreak as the woman breezed by.

Her heart went out to her, but it gave her courage, too. There was still a chance for her. She repeated it over and over in her mind.

A thin woman in skinny jeans and a clipboard took the stage. Into her headset microphone, she said, "Next up is Melanie Drake."

She pointed to a man in the orchestra pit operating a panel of controls. He turned a knob, pressed a lever, and Melanie's music began.

Fear and excitement traveled through her with the rhythm. This was it.

After two deep breaths, she smiled and stepped out of the wings, slinking, swaying, and letting the music lead her. Trying to forget that the rest of her life depended on the next three minutes.

She concentrated on the music, forcing herself to follow it instead of anticipating it, but then the music was its own reminder. Every drum beat a reminder of him.

Don't think about that now!

Her fake smile faltered. She'd been so sure she would see him today, so sure what had gone wrong could be made right again.

She stretched her smile. She had to focus.

The truth was, she was nervous about seeing him, but knowing she might never see him again was so much worse.

To know that it was because of her, because of her idiocy, it was almost too much to bear.

She stumbled a step and tried to recover.

"Sorry," she said aloud, as if that mattered.

Focus!

She couldn't help but think *he* should be here. He loved this show. He loved this world and the music.

But so did she, a defiant part of herself insisted. She should be here, too. She deserved to be.

No. A week ago, maybe. Two or three weeks ago, definitely. Not now. She couldn't do it, if it was only because she had taken it away from him.

She loved him.

She froze. The music continued, but she wasn't following it anymore. She stared helplessly into the darkness beyond the spotlight's glare. In the wings, Skinny Jeans was whispering furiously into her headset and staring at her.

The woman waved her hands. When that didn't work, she marched toward Melanie. "What is the problem?"

"I have to say something." The words came out meek and thin, and they were nearly lost in the music.

Skinny Jeans turned to the audio guy and made a slashing motion at her throat. The music stopped.

"I have something to say," Melanie said again, more boldly this time to the faceless people she knew were sitting in the sixth row.

From the look on Skinny Jeans, she may as well have said there were Martians crawling in the curtains.

Skinny Jeans turned blankly to the bright abyss and waited for direction.

Melanie shielded her eyes with her hands and could make out three silhouettes. Garrett Sheffield had to be one of them.

"Hello?" she offered tentatively. "I need to say something about Taz Roman."

Skinny Jeans reached for her, probably to drag her offstage. Melanie pulled away.

Taz's name seemed to silence all the chatter in the room, all the ambient noise. Melanie knew every eye in the theater was now riveted on her.

Every instinct told her to stop. She was ruining any chance to ever get into the troupe.

Still, Taz didn't deserve what she had done to him, and it certainly shouldn't have cost him his job. Worse, it had cost him his music, and just when he was preparing to launch his own solo album. If only he had said something.

Why hadn't he asked her to set the record straight? Why had he shut her out?

It didn't matter. This was the right thing to do. She could learn to live with never being a Belly Dance Diva. She could never live with what she'd done to Taz.

"Mr. Sheffield," she began, "there are some things being said about Taz that aren't true."

She paused and waited in the spotlight's glare for some kind of permission to continue. There was only silence and the thrumming of blood beating in her ears.

She cleared her throat and continued. "That blog said Taz was trading special treatment in the Divas' audition for favors."

She could hardly believe she was saying these things. It was as if all the blood in her body was swimming around in her head, drowning her.

"And…" said a familiar British voice in the darkness.

"None of it's true."

"How do you know?"

"Because I'm the one who said it."

There were audible gasps from backstage. She spun around and saw dancers gathered in the wings, listening to everything.

It didn't matter. She had to say it. She had to tell the truth.

"I'm the source they didn't name. I was angry and frustrated when I said it, and I didn't mean it. He never did anything wrong while we were together."

"While you were together?"

Crap. Why had she said that? "It's not what you think. I was just living at his house because he wanted me to pretend to be his girlfriend so his sister would leave him alone."

Oh, God! She was babbling. She should just shut up.

"So it was a platonic arrangement?"

She envisioned Taz in the bed beside her. And beneath her. Could they see her cheeks burning red?

"Mostly," she mumbled.

She could hear the tittering behind her, and her face burned hotter.

"Look," she said, "he needed a fake girlfriend, and I was available. I asked him to coach me. That wasn't his idea, initially."

Spilling her guts like this had passed the point of being mortifying. She was almost numb. And now that she'd begun this awkward confession, she couldn't stop.

"I've wanted to be a Belly Dance Diva forever. It's my dream, and I've never wanted anything as badly as I want this. I thought I'd be crazy to pass up the opportunity to have someone like Taz Roman help me. The thing is, even when he agreed, I didn't really believe I could do it. He changed that. He made me believe in myself. But he never, ever promised something inappropriate. He never promised to get me in the troupe."

She stopped. Her chest heaved, and her breath was short. Her throat collapsed in some phantom death grip. She wanted to run, but there was still more to say.

"The day I said what I did, I was angry. I was hurt. The fact was, I was jealous. I was an idiot and thought Taz's help meant something more than it did. It's so embarrassing to admit now, but I thought he was interested in me. He never was. He was always very clear about where we stood with each other. I was the one who made the mistake, not him. When I realized my mistake, I lashed out. I just wanted to vent. I never meant for it to hurt anyone, especially him. What people are saying about him now, it just isn't true. He's a good guy, he's a great drummer, and he doesn't deserve what happened. He deserves to be in the show, not me."

She paused and waited for someone to say something. The audio guy dropped a CD case, and the clatter shot through the hall. Even the woman with the headset stood silent.

So, that was it. There was nothing else to say.

She searched the blackness again. The three silhouettes didn't move.

"Thank you for your time," she said. "I'm sorry for all of it." With her eyes on the stage floor, she hurried off the stage and collected her bag.

The spiky-haired guy was walking toward her as she headed for the door.

"How'd it go?" he asked cheerfully.

"I'm sure you'll hear all about it," she grumbled.

"Oh," he said in that way that really means "I'm sorry I asked."

Melanie didn't go directly to the parking garage. She didn't hold her head high or try to pretend she was fine. What she did was slip into the women's restroom, hole herself up in a stall, and when she was sure she was completely alone, she cried like a little girl. Like the day her mother told her that her father had moved out.

She cried until the hurt washed away—for the audition, for her mother, for her life. She cried until she couldn't possibly cry another tear. She cried until she was just plain tired of crying. The hardest part was, no one else had made this mess. Taz had played his part, but this was her mess. She owned it, and she would deal with it.

When she emerged from the stall, she checked the damage in the mirror. Eyeliner smeared around her eyes and in rivulets down her cheek. Lipstick smudged all around her mouth. Her teal rose hairpin had slid down to her neck.

She laughed. Just a chuckle at first, but then it was a full, belly laugh she couldn't stop. She looked like one of those devil-possessed clowns in a hacker film. She looked like a hot, stinking mess.

It was funny, though, even if it was her life.

She pulled two paper towels from the dispenser, wet them, and went to work cleaning up the worst of the damage. Makeup, hair, attitude—when it was all in better order, she peeked into the lobby.

Still empty. She hurried across the floor and slipped out one of the glass doors. The sun was high in the sky and bright. Bright enough to scatter the shadows that still lingered at the edge of her thoughts. She didn't know where she was going. It didn't matter. She'd figure it out when she got behind the wheel. Maybe Laguna for a walk along Main Beach. Maybe the Huntington Pier.

Oh, who was she kidding? She knew exactly where she was going. She was going to that pile of blankets on Abby's living room sofa. She was going to crawl beneath them and maybe never come out.

CHAPTER FORTY-FIVE

THE STUDIO'S BOUTIQUE door opened, but Melanie kept her eyes on the bills in her hand, and counted to herself, "Twenty-five, thirty, thirty-five, forty—"

"Here you go, the biggest cup—"

Melanie's hand flew up to halt Abby's words.

"Forty-five, fifty, fifty-five. There, done." She looked up. "Sorry. What did you say?"

Abby set a big cup of coffee beside the cash register. "Don't let me interrupt you. I haven't seen you this focused since…"

Melanie knew why Abby let the comment die. It wasn't exactly a sore subject. It was just one they didn't mention. Not since Melanie quit the newspaper and asked for the boutique manager job. That was more than two weeks ago now, and it was becoming easier not to think about it.

Abby regrouped and started again. "Have I mentioned lately how glad I am you're here?"

Melanie pretended to mull it over. "Uh, probably not since yesterday."

"It's just because I know you gave up a lot to do it, and it means the world to me. I'm good with students, and I'm pretty good with numbers, but I have to admit, this retail stuff is harder than it looks." She glanced around at the new hip scarves that needed to be folded and the messy skirt rack.

"I'm happy to keep it in shape for you," Melanie said. "It's a lot more fun than running month-end financial reports for Deffner or making sure he doesn't miss his weekly status meetings." She stepped back from the case and presented her outfit. "And where else could I wear yoga pants and a stretch choli to work, or not worry about whether my ink shows. Not to mention all the free studio time."

"Yep, as much free studio time as you want. You can practice to your heart's content. By next year, when auditions come around again, they won't know what hit 'em."

Melanie looked away. Abby was trying to be helpful, she knew that. It didn't diminish the sting. She swallowed hard, looked back, and tried to make light of it. "Well, I appreciate your optimism, but we both know *that's* not going to happen. I had my chance." She wanted to add, "and I blew it," but the words wouldn't come. Instead, she changed the subject. "I figure I'll work on trying to pick up a few private-lesson students then see what happens."

"Maybe get your own place? You must be miserable being back at your mom's."

"Actually, I'm not. Things between us are better than they've ever been."

"That's great," Abby said. "If you ever want to come back to my place, you can do that, too. I liked having you there."

Before Melanie could respond, the bell jingled, and the studio door opened.

Taz filled the doorway. Not smirking and cocky as he had been that first day. He stood at the threshold with his fists in the front pockets of his jeans. Almost timid. Almost boyish. As though he wasn't sure he was welcome.

CHAPTER FORTY-SIX

MELANIE JUST STARED. As if Taz were a ghost. A memory of better days.

"Hi, Taz," Abby said with forced enthusiasm. "Great to see you. Right, Melanie?"

"Yeah," Melanie managed to say.

"Hi," he said sheepishly, avoiding eye contact. He ran antsy fingers through his hair, which was pulled back in a ponytail. It looked like he wanted to say more, but his mouth tensed, and he stayed silent.

For a long moment, no one said anything, and tension stretched between them like a taut rubber band.

"You know," Abby continued, drawing out the words, filling up time. "I need to check on something in the back. Will you excuse me?" With her eyes, she motioned to Melanie as if to ask, "Are you okay? Do you have this?"

Melanie nodded, but she honestly didn't know. She didn't know anything.

"Holler if you need anything," Abby said, and she disappeared around the corner.

Taz moved closer.

"I heard you were working here. I hope you don't mind me just showing up. Maybe I should have called. I probably should have called."

Melanie couldn't watch him shift and fidget. It was so not like him. Stripped of his confidence, it was like it wasn't even Taz anymore, and it made her want to do crazy things, like throw her arms around him and comfort him. She wanted to nuzzle her nose in that warm, tender part of his neck.

Stop! What was she thinking? She stared hard at the unpaired earrings. The mix of gold and silver chains in front of her. She had to focus on something else. What had she been doing? Why couldn't she think? "No," she said. "It's fine."

He took another step closer. "Look," he said, "I owe you an apology."

Her glance shot up from the merchandise to meet his gaze squarely for the first time. "No," she practically shouted before getting a grip on herself. "If anything, I owe you an apology. A big one, and I know it. What those bloggers said... what I said, I guess... I didn't mean it. I was angry and hurt and stupid."

"You weren't stupid. It was my own fault. You know, I didn't realize it till later, but I went out with one of those girls. The blond one. It was just once last year, and I didn't even remember until she called the day after that post. She wanted to know if she could come over for an interview, to get my side of the story. When I said no, she went ballistic. She brought up how I hadn't called her after our date, and how I blew her off." He shrugged. "She's right. It was a dick move. Guess she showed me, huh?"

He chuckled, but the humor didn't reach his eyes.

She curled her fingers into fists, fighting the urge to jump to his defense.

He didn't pause for long, though. "I know I put you in an awkward position. I never should have taken it so far. I guess I wanted to believe you wanted to be with me." He sighed and threw his head back. "I don't know what I was thinking. Of course you must have thought that was part of the bargain. You have to believe me, that was never my intention."

"I know," she blurted. "That's not why I did it." She winced, trying to wrap her mind around what he just said. "So you think I'm mad at you?"

"Well, yeah," he scoffed. "Aren't you? I mean, you have a right to be."

Her head swam with confusion. It felt like the world just turned upside down. "No," she said. "I'm the one at fault. I'm the one who opened my big mouth to those girls. I'm the one who got jealous."

"Jealous?" he cut in. "Of what?"

"Tamara. It was obvious you still care for her."

"Whoa, hold on," he said and covered his eyes with his hands, squeezing his brow. "You thought I wanted to be with her?"

"Well, yeah. You two looked very cozy at the party."

He shook his head. "That was not what was happening. That will never happen. We had some unfinished business, yeah, and my sister had told her some things that were misleading, to say the least. I just needed a minute to clear it up. That's why I was talking to her. That's the only reason. If you had stayed, you would have seen that she left about ten minutes after you did."

"But she was at your house."

He shook his head. "Gina's doing. Not mine. Like I said, she didn't stay. Is that the only reason you left?"

He was standing at the display case now, across from her. She could see his hands, the curly, blond hair on his wrists and arms. She flashed on the moment those hands had been in her hair and roaming over her skin.

He was waiting for an answer. She had the feeling he would stand there, staring at her until he got one.

"Yeah," she said with a shrug. "Okay, so it was all just a misunderstanding."

She wanted to leave it at that, but she knew she couldn't. She was being honest now, which meant she had to be totally honest.

"Look, I lost my temper. I never meant for those things I said to those girls to be taken the way they were. I had no idea what had happened until it was too late."

He smiled a meek smile. She knew what he was thinking: It didn't make things better.

"I never meant for you to get fired, Taz. I absolutely never wanted that to happen."

The truth of that tore through her. She couldn't help but think how she would feel if someone had taken her passion—her dancing—away from her.

That's what she had done to him. That's why she didn't deserve to be a Belly Dance Diva.

He was staring at the floor again. When he finally glanced up, he said, "I wasn't fired. That rumor started, and I didn't correct it. But the truth is, I quit."

CHAPTER FORTY-SEVEN

MELANIE INSTANTLY FELT the questions mounting. She wanted to know what he meant. She wanted him to explain. Honestly, how was it even possible?

The only sound she could muster was, "Huh?"

"Things got really complicated," he said with a sigh. "Gina convinced herself Garrett was taking advantage of our partnership. I told her she was wrong, but she wouldn't listen. I tried to tell her it was my choice, that I didn't want to be involved in the business side of things, that I liked things the way they were."

"Then why would you quit?"

"That night, after you left the Pandemonium, she told me she got a lawyer. She said she was going to file a lawsuit saying I had no right to use the money I invested with Garrett without her permission."

"Her permission? But isn't half the money yours?"

He shook his head like the whole matter disgusted him. "She found some piece of paper, some stupid contract I'd signed years ago giving her power of attorney because she was managing the money in the beginning. She told me I never officially rescinded it, so it was technically still in effect."

Melanie didn't know much about the law, but she could see by the look on his face it was bad. "I'm sorry. That sucks."

"She said she was going to get my money back from Garrett, whether I liked it or not. So before she could cost us all a bundle in legal fees and embarrass the hell out of me, I quit and asked Garrett to buy me out. I figured I'd lose the show, but at least I'd have money to buy my dad's masters from his old record label, and I could finally finish the legacy album. Now I own them. They're mine." He smiled, for the first time since he walked through the door.

"You went to New York?" Hope surged within her, but just for a moment. He still could have called. It wasn't like the city had no cell service.

"Yeah," he said. "It took a few meetings with the label guys, but I got them to release the recordings. It wasn't easy, but I got them."

"I guess you must have been pretty busy these past couple of weeks, then." She winced. Why did she have to say that? She might as well wave a flag that said, "Look how pitiful I am." She hurried to add, "So all those rumors, all the gossip about you being fired. It was just completely wrong?"

"It was easier to let it run its course. I figured it would die down eventually, and it wouldn't matter, anyway if I wasn't with the show." He chuckled. "And since I lost my phone, it was *really* easy to ignore."

"You lost your phone?" Hope reared its head again.

"It's all right. I found it, or rather, Gina found it. In the driveway after I left. I must have dropped it as I was leaving. Luckily, she relayed messages to me at the hotel. She wasn't thrilled about having to be my secretary for a few days, though."

"Emails too, huh?" She knew she was being obvious, but she couldn't help herself.

"She had to forward all of it to me." He laughed. "Well, she was supposed to relay it all. Turns out, she left a few things out."

She wanted to ask about hers. Was it one that didn't make it through? The question couldn't get past her throat.

An awkward silence stretched between them.

"I'm really happy things worked out for you," she said at last, knowing it wasn't the right thing to say. It was true, but it was nowhere near what she wanted to tell him.

He shook his head like he was shaking off his own doubts. "I didn't come here to tell you all that. That's not why I'm here." He glanced up and met her gaze. "I came to thank you."

Did she hear that wrong?

She must have looked utterly confused, because he quickly added, "Garrett has been trying to reach me ever since your audition, but my sister never told me. We didn't connect until yesterday, when I got back."

Panic stabbed at her. "What did my audition have to do with anything?"

"I never told him why I wanted to leave the show. I figured it was best if he just thought I wanted to do my dad's album. It turns out I should have talked to him, because he's got a lawyer who says that document Gina was holding over my head would never hold up in court."

"That's good news."

"Yeah, no doubt."

"But I still don't see what that has to do with my audition."

It was his turn to look sheepish. "Garrett only started to question why I quit because of what you said to him."

She pulled back.

"He told you what I said?"

"Of course he did. Wouldn't you tell your friend?"

He had a point. She shrugged.

"At first he assumed it was because of that blog post. He tried telling me he didn't believe it and not to worry about it. He couldn't understand why I still wanted to quit. He said he couldn't believe it was just the legacy album, and the only other answer he could come up with was that you dumped me after Pandemonium and the Tamara fiasco, and I was taking it badly. After your audition, he realized that wasn't it either. That's when he started tracking me down again. When I told him I was trying to protect him and the show from Gina, he got his lawyer on the phone."

Her heart and head were pounding. It all made sense, but there was still one thing—one person—he hadn't mentioned. The question eked out of her. "What about Tamara?"

He gave her a look like she'd just jumped aboard the crazy train.

"She was at your house," she added. "You looked like you were back together."

"What? No. My sister invited her over, but she didn't stay. I left after you did, and she was gone when I got back. We are not getting back together. Not now, not ever."

"What about Gina?"

"She's gone, too. Thankfully." He sighed. "I would never admit this to her, but in some ways, my sister was right about some things. There is more to life than drumming and performing. I don't need her to tell me how to live my life, but I know, in the end, she has my best interests at heart."

He stopped and shook his head. "But I've gotten completely off track again. What I came to say, what I came to ask, actually, is would you still consider joining the Belly Dance Divas?"

"Oh, right," she scoffed. "Like I'm ever going to stand up in front of those judges again."

"No, you won't," he said.

It wasn't said with malice, but the words sliced through her. She dropped her glance again so he wouldn't see the tears welling in her eyes. She blinked fast, forcing them back. She forced back the lump creeping up her throat.

He must have known emotion was getting the best of her, because he stepped toward her and put his hand on her arm.

Oh, crap. Now she was playing the pity card, even though that was the last thing she wanted to do. *Get a grip, Mel. Stop acting like a baby.*

"You won't," he said, his voice quiet and consoling. "At least I hope you won't. Damn, this is harder than I thought it would be. See, the thing is, I need a partner in the show."

"The show? But you quit. What about your album?"

"I did quit, and I am going to do the album. That's what I've been trying to tell you. Garrett made me an offer. He said he respects the fact that I want to cut back my involvement in the show, but that it doesn't have to be all or nothing. He asked if I'd like to stay on as partner and do just one drum solo per show. In exchange, I get to keep my stake in the show, and he'll help me promote the album when it's done."

"But I thought you used the money to buy the masters."

He sighed again. "Yeah, I did. But I really wanted back in the show, so I found the money."

"*Found* money?"

He pulled a jumble of keys out of his front pocket and clicked a key fob. The lights on an old, weather-beaten, soft-top Jeep flashed in the parking lot.

"Sheila's gone?"

He nodded. "Sitting pretty in a tax lawyer's Newport Beach garage."

He was smiling, but she could see the pain on his face. That breakup was going to sting for a while.

"It sounds like everything worked out, then," she said. It really was great. It was everything he wanted, even if it meant giving up his most prized possession.

"I get it now. You wanted me to know you're fine. That despite my big mouth, I didn't ruin your life."

"No, that's not it at all." He took her hands and held them both. "Garrett said he wanted me to pick a dancer to dance during the solo. He said I could pick anybody."

The air changed. The ground tilted.

"What are you saying?"

He stroked her fingers with his thumbs. "What I'm saying—what I'm asking is—will you dance with me?"

"Are you joking? This isn't funny if this is some kind of joke."

She tried to wrap her mind around what he was offering, but it was too good to be true. It was impossible. "So I'd be onstage with you, performing while you played?"

He nodded, and a smile slid across his face.

"I would be, like, a real Belly Dance Diva?"

He shook his head. "No, you wouldn't be *like* a real Belly Dance Diva." He lifted her chin with his finger. "You would *be* a Belly Dance Diva."

His green eyes shimmered.

Her body went numb. Her mind reeled. "I would be a Belly Dance Diva," she said emphatically. "I would be dancing with you in every show on the tour?"

"Every show."

It was all so wonderful. All so unbelievable. She had so many questions. One stood out above the others. It was simple, and it was important. It was simply this:

"Why me?"

He smiled the sweetest smile she'd ever seen. "It's because you get it. You get the music and the rhythm and the feel of it. You get it, just like I get it. When I played for you at the Tent, it was like nothing I'd ever experienced with another dancer. It was like we had a connection. I think I fell in love with you right then and there."

"You did?"

He chuckled. "Yeah, it surprised me, too. I didn't want to, and then I didn't want to admit it, not even to myself. I think that's why it was so easy to push you away. Why I push everyone away. I didn't want to be in that place where I was... where I could be hurt again. I felt like I had done that already, and it hadn't worked so why try again. Especially when it was really obvious you didn't feel the same way—"

"But I did," she blurted. "I mean, I do feel the same way." She threw herself into his arms, wrapping her own around his neck and holding him like she was never going to let him go.

The shock of it surprised him, but slowly she felt his arms drape over her, his hands working their way through her hair.

She stared at him, and he stared back with love in his eyes.

"Are you sure?" he asked, tentative and almost choked with emotion.

"I've never been more sure of anything in my life."

She proved it with a big kiss on his lips.

EPILOGUE

THE RED-VELVET curtain of the La Regina Playhouse rose to reveal Taz Roman bare-chested but for a Bedouin-style vest and sitting on a stool, a microphone angled over his lap to catch every brush and slap of his *doumbek*. A few taps with his fingertips, then a rapid trill and the drum solo of the Los Angeles premiere of the Belly Dance Divas' summer world tour was underway.

From the wings, a dancer appeared, covered in shimmering silver except where her tattoos played peekaboo through the draped layers of fringe scarves, bangles, and beads. At the sight of her, the sold-out crowd erupted in applause.

As the music played, it seemed to move through her. Her hips swayed, her arms and wrists floated and circled around her. And it lured her closer to Taz. To his languorous beat, she slinked and slithered toward him, like a serpent to her charmer.

"Melanie looks gorgeous up there," gushed Janaya in the box seat she shared with Abby. "They both do. It's like they've been dancing together forever. Like one of those classic couples, you know, Fred and Ginger, Judy and Mickey, and..." Her expression twisted in thought, trying to pull more names from memory.

"Samia and Farid?" Abby offered.

"Yes! Exactly. It's so romantic, don't you think?"

They watched Melanie circle in front of Taz, her eyes never leaving his, his never leaving hers. It was impossible to know whether it was her body leading him or his music leading her. They moved in perfect unison.

She dipped her hip and flashed him a coy glance. He played back, pausing a beat, making her wonder, then raced through the rhythm until she caught up. The sexy flirtation playing out onstage mesmerized the audience. When she laid a soft hand on his shoulder and trailed it along his arm, every rear in the house shifted in its seat, feeling that visceral connection.

"You know what this means, don't you?" Abby asked, not looking away, and smiling ear to ear with the happiness she could feel from her friend radiating from the stage.

"Of course I do," Janaya shot back. "For the next four weeks, I have to cover Melanie's classes and probably the boutique, too. You know what that's going to do to my social life?"

Abby laughed. "Yeah, there's that, but what I meant was, you're probably next."

"Next what?"

"Next to fall in love."

"Oh, no way," Janaya said, waving away the idea. "That might be fine for you and Melanie, but I am not interested."

"Yeah," Abby said with a sly grin. "I've heard that before."

THE END

***

Thank you for reading *Dance with Me*. You can find out what happens next with Taz and Melanie in *Another Dance*, a sexy short story in the California Belly Dance Romance series. Learn more at www.DeAnnaCameron.com/book-three.

AUTHOR'S NOTE

Thank you for taking the time to read *Dance with Me*.

If you enjoyed it, please consider leaving a review at your favorite e-retailer or Goodreads.com. Your support makes a real difference and would be truly appreciated.

***

Have you read all the books in the *California Belly Dance Romance* series?

Shimmy for Me (Book 1)
Dance with Me (Book 2)
Another Dance (Book 3)
Jingly Bells (Book 4)

Visit www.DeAnnaCameron.com for details

ACKNOWLEDGMENTS

I'd like to thank some special people who contributed in important ways to this book:

The members of the Extraordinary Readers Club: Jasmine Talbert, Ann Johnson, Nikki, Laura, Christina, Jennifer, Michelle, Shannon, Abigail, Clarissa, and Tracy. I'm endlessly grateful to these amazing people for their help and support.

The O.C. Writers, a constant source of camaraderie and inspiration. And especially Greta Boris, my partner in crime.

My parents, Rod and Elida, and Alice and Lou, whose love and encouragement never fails.

My Chloe, who at six is already a more prolific writer than her mommy, and I couldn't be prouder.

And finally Austin, my very own, swoonworthy hero.